In Hiding

A Crime Novel

PRAISE FOR TIMOTHY SHEARD'S NOVELS!

This Won't Hurt A Bit - "...outraged staff members go to their union representative, a scrappy custodian named Lenny Moss, and ask him to find the real killer. Since there's no merit to the case against the laundry worker to begin with, Lenny is just wasting his time. But Sheard, a veteran nurse, makes sure that readers do not waste theirs. His intimate view of Lenny's world is a gentle eyeopener into the way a large institution looks from a workingman's perspective." **New York Times**

Sheard's stories draw readers into the thick of things and keep them enthralled all the way to the end. Because he's an RN, he knows all the appropriate hospital lingo and hurls it around in a way that gives the series not only heft but authenticity. Plus, he comes up with an excellent ending. **Labor Notes**

Some Cuts Never Heal - "This well-plotted page-turner is guaranteed to scare the bejesus out of anyone anticipating a hospital stay anytime in the near future." **Publishers Weekly**

"Sheard supplies...polished prose and elements of warmth and humor. Strongly recommended for most mystery collections." **Library Journal**

A Race Against Death - "Timothy Sheard provides a delightful hospital investigative tale that grips readers from the moment that Dr. Singh and his team apply CPR, but fail." **Mysteries Galore**

Slim To None - "Here's a page flipper, a murder mystery set in a hospital where the invisible, everyday workers are the key...a great read, a complicated mystery, good friends, comradeship in hard times, and union workers shown in full humanity. Get it now!" Earl Silbar, AFSCME 3506, City Colleges of Chicago

No Place To Be Sick - "...there's enough suspense, fear and chills running up and down your spine to make you keep on reading it in one fell sweep. Watch your back if you're alone in the house!" **Pride and a Paycheck**

"Find out if Lenny & his friends win their battle in this roller coaster of a story." **Union Communications**

A Bitter Pill - "There are plenty of twists and turns, all with the quiet force of intense realism, as anyone who has worked in health care, or even been a hospital patient, can tell." **Labor Notes**

"It doesn't take long for Moss...to begin digging, and his efforts to unravel this mystery are highly entertaining. In addition, they add intrigue and drama to an already complex and layered story." **Truthout**

"...a short, fast, tight book, giving us what we like best about Lenny Moss, hospital custodian and union steward." **UALE DIGEST**

Love Dies - "By turns creepy and compassionate, this well-plotted summer release is entertaining, eerie, and unsettling." **Brooklyn Examiner**

"This is an exciting thriller starring an intriguing doctor, an ailing first responder and a for hire mercenary killer...with an amusing lampooning of the book publishing industry to lighten the dark story line of what happens when literally Love Dies." **Mystery Gazette**

For Siobhan and Julian

Wishing you a joyful life together.

I want a love that doesn't know my past,
That looks upon my scars and is not
inclined to ask.
Loving a man like me is no easy task.
I know she's somewhere
Counting the stars
With me.

Counting the Stars, Christopher Sheard

Published by Hard Ball Press, March, 2014.
Information available at: www.hardballpress.com
ISBN: 978-0-9911639-0-8

Cover art courtesy of Julian Thorpe
Book design by D. Bass.

In Hiding

A Crime Novel

By Timothy Sheard

ONE

Cripes, it's nine-thirty in the morning already. Angie should be up and awake and getting ready for work but there's no sign of life. Her bedroom light's off and her curtains are closed. She always opens her curtains in the morning and looks up at the sky and down at the street, like she doesn't trust the weather forecast. Like she's looking for a sign how her day is gonna go.

Or her life.

Could be she's sick, she's looked a little drawn lately coming home from work. The other night her mouth was set in a line as she entered the building and she walked kind of bent over like she was weighed down by some gloomy thoughts. I hope she's okay; I hope it's nothing serious.

I'll give her till ten-thirty. If she's not up by then she'll be late for work. Her boss at Artistry is a churlish little bastard. Angie should never have left Snips down on the Bowery and gone to work at that fancy-shmancy hair salon. I guess the money's better uptown. A lot of her customers changed salons to stay with her; that says a lot about what kind of girl she is.

Come on, Angie, shake a leg. Look out your window at the wakening sky and see your future in the clouds, the way I see my future in your eyes.

Dammit! It's eleven already and Angie still hasn't opened her curtains. Wish I could keep watch at the window all morning but I've got to get some sleep, I worked all night on that QuickTime video for the new *Wrestling Women* site and it's still jerky as hell. God save the poor schmuck watching on a cell phone, those 4G connections are a bunch of bull; half the time they download at 2G. The wrestling matches will look like those old hand-cranked nickel shorts from a hundred years ago, and the client's gonna blame *me* for the poor quality streaming.

Maybe she left last night for a little vacation. It's only fair, as hard as she works, six days a week cutting hair for those hotshot professionals in the three-piece suits. She should chill out on a cruise ship somewhere, letting some gay guy cut her hair and color and style it. Every three, four months she changes her hair and gets a whole new look, letting a new gal practice on her. That's my Angie: always willing to help out a newcomer. She should get a bonus.

When I woke up this evening and looked across the street at Angie's apartment the sun was glinting off the windows but the curtains were still closed. No sign of life at all. Is she sleeping over at some guy's? I guess I'll have to run up to Artistry and see is she at work. It would mean going *in* the place, and if she *was* there she would see me, but I don't know what else to do, I've got to know she's all right.

I jumped on the Lexington Avenue train to the Lenox Hill stop and stood across the street watching the place. I used the telephoto on my camera to get a good look. After an hour there was still no sign of Angie. The chair she always uses was empty. Her leather jacket with the top button that doesn't *exactly* match the others wasn't hanging on its hook, and it's a warm day, so if she went out for a bite she probably would have left her jacket on the hook.

I chewed on the situation for awhile, weighing the pros and cons, debating whether to go into the place. Being noticed is *never* a good idea. But there was no other way, so I went inside for a haircut. They had classical music playing softly, plush velvet armchairs to sit in and wait, and herbal teas on a little marble table. Even the paper cups were classy.

I looked around the room for any sign that Angie was there, but didn't see anything that belonged to her. A slim, dark haired young woman in skin tight leather pants came to the counter and asked if she could help me. Her name tag read Eglantine. She had milk chocolate skin and pink lips.

"Last time I was here Angie cut my hair. Is she working tonight?"

"No, sir, Angie is not here." She spoke in a soft Caribbean accent that was lilting and musical.

As she turned away from me I said, "Could you cut my hair?"

"If you wish." Enthusiasm wasn't her thing.

She led me back to a leather and chrome seat where she told me to park my butt. As I dropped into the chair she wrapped a bib around my neck. "What is your style?"

"Gee, I don't really have one."

"I can see that." She sprayed water on my head. The water ran down my neck.

"How about cutting it so there's just enough to part?"

She stepped back and surveyed my head. "A part in the middle is a conservative look. I see you as more hip. Straight back with no part."

"Yeah, that sounds good."

I settled back and let her start snipping. She worked away, turning my head to the side or bending it back as if I were a department store mannequin.

"I didn't see you the last time Angie cut my hair. Have you worked at Artistry long?"

"A couple of months." When she bent low I sniffed her perfume. It smelled like exotic flowers.

"That's a pretty name, Eglantine. Where is it from?"

"It is the name of an English flower. I am from Nevis. Do you know of it?"

"Oh, sure. It was colonized by the Brits, wasn't it?"

"Yes, but we have been independent for many years."

After letting Eglantine work for a while, I said in a casual voice, "She's a real art lover, that Angie. She's always going to galleries and museums. You've probably heard her talking about it."

Snip, snip. Eglantine continued working without comment.

I pointed to a charcoal drawing on the wall. "Is that one of her drawings?"

"I just cut hair, sir. I don't know about art."

"Angie mentioned she was going to an exhibition this month somewhere in Tribeca. I sure wish I —*ouch!*"

Eglantine poked my ear with the tip of her scissors just hard enough to not break the skin. "I myself like Van Gogh," she said.

The churlish little manager, a sweaty guy in a cheap wig, came over and whispered something in Eglantine's ear. She shook her head no and went on cutting my hair, while the manager went to the counter and watched us with his beady little ferret eyes.

When she was done, Eglantine ripped the apron from around my neck without offering me a look at my neck. "No mirror for the back?" I asked.

"What for? *You* don't see it."

Admitting she had a point, I paid her with a decent tip and headed for the door. In the reflection in the window I saw the manager staring at my back as if he wanted to sink a knife into it. I've been watching people all my life, and I can tell when somebody's got good intentions and when they're evil, and this guy could bottle evil and sell it to the mob. I was glad he didn't know who I was.

As I looked back from the sidewalk I saw the manager go up to Eglantine, put a thick hand on her shoulder and say something. Eglantine's face lost her calm self-assurance. As she nodded her head yes there was fear in her eyes.

Back in my apartment I wondered where to look next. Angie doesn't have a lot of friends. Sometimes a girl stays over at her place for a few nights and I never see her again. Could be Angie's a lesbian, which would be okay with me. In fact, it'd be cool. I could still love her, only ours would be a platonic sort of love, which is the purest kind, really.

Last week she went out to dinner with a girl from her old job at Snips. Tasha. They ate at a Thai joint. Angie ordered coconut soup and grilled fish; Tasha had dumplings with dipping sauce and pad thai. Angie smiled a lot and laughed a bunch of times. It was nice. I was happy for her. After dinner they went to an art gallery in NoHo. It's good having a friend. I'm glad I have Angie.

Before getting back to my work on the computer I studied Angie's apartment through the telescope. There didn't seem to be any change. The curtain was still closed, except... the curtain wasn't as tightly closed as it had been in the morning. There was a slender V-shaped gap from the top of the window two-thirds down. I would have been able to see a sliver of the apartment inside if the lights were on. Angie always leaves a night light on.

It looked like she'd been there and gone. She probably came back for a change of clothes. Fresh panties and socks.

Up 'til now I'd been worried was she okay. Now I was partly relieved, seeing she'd been back to the apartment, and partly jealous. I wanted to see the face of whoever was keeping time with her. I wanted to know that Angie was with somebody who made her laugh and treated her like royalty, because that's what she deserved.

Sitting down at my computer, I asked myself, how am I going to get any work done if I have to keep one eye glued to the telescope *all night?*

TWO

I worked for about an hour on the Wrestling Women web program, trying not to think about what Angie was doing, when Marty called. He lives in the loft upstairs.

"Hey, Pete. We need a new cable for the video projector, ours has a short. Any chance we could borrow one for the movie tonight?"

I told him no problem, I'd bring one up to them. I grabbed a spare VGA cable and went upstairs to the loft. His apartment is on the top floor of the building and opens right onto the roof. Marty was outside stretching a white sheet across a homemade wooden frame; his girlfriend Becka was in the kitchen cooking something spicy.

I asked Marty how was the ambulance work going. He's the lean, rugged type with dirty blonde hair who looks great in his EMT uniform. I'd look like Beetle Bailey if I ever put something like that on.

"I had a *great* run today! A woman got drunk and fell and smashed her face up and there was buckets of blood pouring out. It took three pressure dressings to control the bleeding."

"That's nice," I said, handing him the cable.

Becka came out on the roof with a plate of crispy sweet potatoes. She walks with this smooth, fluid gait, as if she were sliding on ice. It makes her ethereal. When I took one she asked, "Would you pay two dollars for a bag of these?"

"Um, I guess so. Can I put ketchup on it?"

Becka's face fell when I asked about ketchup. "The only reason you use ketchup is 'cause most french fries are made from frozen pieces of crap that have no flavor and zero nutrition." She held up a sweet potato. "I'm using unpeeled organic sweet potatoes. I brush them with olive oil and paprika and bake them 'til they're lightly browned."

I felt like an idiot and tried to think of some way to apologize, but the words got stuck in my throat. I get flustered sometimes when Becka's around. Well, more like all the time she's near me, she's so damn beautiful.

Marty popped a potato crisp in his mouth. "Sublime," he said with a wry smile. He's got that Clint Eastwood, understated way about him.

I watched Becka as she set down the tray of food and turned to go back to the kitchen, walking in that silky way she has. In the light from the video reflected off the sheet her pale freckled face was as beautiful as the girl with a pearl earring in the Vermeer painting. That Marty is one lucky guy.

As I turned to go, Marty asked if I would come back later for the movie. I told him I might stop by later, but knew I wouldn't, I'm not comfortable in crowds. I like to sit in the last row of a movie theater and watch the patrons reacting to the movie more than I look at the film.

I worked on the *Wrestling Women* video for a few more hours. Around nine-thirty I got the clips to play clean and sharp. The work was slow because I kept getting up from the computer and looking over at Angie's building. I did a double take when I saw a light come on in her living room window. *At last!* She's home and okay, thank god.

I sharpened the focus of the telescope trying to see into Angie's apartment through the slit in the curtains. Watching people is better than watching a movie or museum exhibit or TV show. I know, I've been watching them my whole life. As long as I can remember I've liked being the guy nobody notices but who sees everything around him.

When I was a little boy I used to hide behind the sofa or the stuffed chair in the corner and watch people who came into the apartment. When mom wanted me to split she'd say in this sing-songy voice, "Come out, come out, wherever you are, Sneaky Pete!" If she said it a second time, she wasn't singing. A third call and I'd get a hard smack to the ear with an open hand that hurt something awful and throbbed all day.

If I came right out from my hiding place she'd give me a quarter and tell me to go to the corner store and get a candy and play in the vacant lot across the street until she called me. I was happy to get the candy. I'd suck a Juicy Fruit and watch people going by. I'd make up stories about who they were and where they were going.

Sometimes I imagined they were taking me with them.

As I looked through the telescope at Angie's window, a figure moved past the slender opening between the curtains. I didn't understand why she didn't open the curtains, her geraniums will wither and die if they don't get some sunlight. Angie killed some daffodils when she first took the apartment, but then she got better and the new plants are doing really great.

I got up and started walking around my apartment. Back and forth. It's a wonder there's no rut down the middle of the floor. I really wanted to know she was okay. I could stay at my post and wait for her to come out of the building or until she opened the curtain, but one minute away to take a leak and I could miss her.

It was time to do a brush by. That's when I pass very close to the person I'm watching without their knowing. It's risky, but it adds aural and olfactory impressions to the visual image. That's a huge plus.

I put on my tool belt, tucked a pair of leather work gloves in my back pocket, put on a corduroy cap, and went across the street to her building. If anybody asked, I'd be an electronics repairman. That's what I know best. Electronics. Computers and televisions and cell phones. Anything with a circuit board, I'm your man.

I waited in front of her building until an old lady with a heavy bag approached the lobby. I pulled the door open for her as soon as she turned the lock. She smiled at me with perfect teeth. They were top quality dentures.

I took the stairs to Angie's floor, walked to her door and listened. I heard a faint rustling sound, then silence. No music or radio or television. Come to think of it, I never saw a television flickering in her apartment. She must be an avid reader.

There was no conversation, so she was either alone or with some guy who was doing the strong silent bit. The peep hole in the door showed light inside the apartment, but I couldn't see through it. Some day I've got to figure a way to look through a peep hole and get it to reveal what's within instead of obscuring it.

I wished I could knock on the door and see her open it, just to be sure she was all right, but that would be crazy. She'd look at me, a complete stranger, wondering what the fuck I was doing bothering her.

I was standing in front of her door not knowing what to do when I heard the lock turn inside. *Holy shit, she was coming out*! My throat started to constrict and my brain froze up. If Angie saw me face to face I'd never be able to follow her again on the subway. Besides, what would I say to her?

I took a step backward trying to decide which way to turn when the door opened and her friend Tasha from Snips appeared in the doorway.

"Can I help you?" she asked, a look of dark distrust on her face. I almost didn't recognize Tasha, she had copper colored hair, not black with silver streaks like the last time I saw her at the restaurant, and her eyebrows were plucked and pencil thin.

"Uh, hi, yeah, I'm, uh, here about the internet connection."

"Excuse me?"

"I have a work order. I understand that Angie . . .Uh, Miss Andrews, has been having trouble with her internet connection for a couple of days. I'm supposed to check it out."

"You work for the *cable company*?" Her look was skeptical.

"Cable? No, I'm a local guy. Here's my card." I reached for my wallet and handed her my business card. "I service a lot of computers in the neighborhood. I live right here on the block. See?"

Tasha studied the card for a long time, as if she was a slow reader. She even turned it over and studied the back, which was blank. I don't know what she expected to see on the back of a business card.

"Angie's out right now. I'm not comfortable letting you in the apartment."

"Sure, I understand. Just ask her to call me when she's in. I'm always home, I work out of my apartment, it's right across the street."

Tasha pocketed the card, closed and locked the door, and went to the elevator. I didn't want to look suspicious, so I joined her for the ride down.

"Will Miss Andrews be home later?" I asked. "I work all night."

"You never know with Angie," said Tasha.

When she answered my question Tasha didn't look me in my eye. You don't have to be a private eye to know when somebody's not being forthcoming.

I walked out with her and crossed the street to my building. At the front door I pretended to search my pockets for my keys and watched her in the reflection on the glass doors. Tasha craned her neck looking up and down the street, then she started walking north, toward the subway station, maybe.

I was tempted to follow her, but she'd seen my face, it would have been impossible. You can't watch somebody who's seen you up close. As long as you stay anonymous, it's really easy to do, especially in New York, a city of strangers. Walk three blocks away from your neighborhood and nobody knows you. You might as well be in another city. Or another country.

All you have to do to watch somebody is to be quiet and unobtrusive. Blend into the scenery and watch from behind a screen or in a reflected surface. Keep your face blank and look bored. Nobody will notice you, even when you're examining someone's every detail.

As Tasha disappeared around a corner, I wondered if Angie was staying with her. Were they lovers or just good friends? Was Angie in trouble? Did she get behind in her rent? She could have lost her job, her chair was empty at Artistry. It was worrisome.

I couldn't stand around waiting for Angie to come back, I had to know she was all right. But since I couldn't follow Tasha home, I had no idea how the hell I was ever going to find my dear Angie.

THREE

After working at the computer late into the night, I fell asleep just as the sky was painting her face purple and pink. The promise of a new day always brings me down, so I usually sleep through the morning.

When I woke up in the afternoon, there was no change in Angie's window. I considered going to Snips where Angie used to work and maybe run into Tasha. I could act like, *Wow, what a coincidence.* Even if she wouldn't talk to me, I might be able to learn Tasha's last name, they post the hairdresser's licenses on the wall, and that should help me track down *her* address, which might lead me to Angie.

I jumped in the shower, turned on the waterproof radio, and listened to the news while I scrubbed away. I wasn't paying much attention until the announcer said that during the night the body of an unidentified young woman had been found in a section of scrub land off Floyd Bennett Field in Brooklyn. They didn't mention her nationality or her features. Normally I wouldn't spend a lot of mental energy thinking about a dead body, but with Angie not coming back to her apartment and Tasha being evasive about Angie's whereabouts, it got me worrying. *What if the dead woman was Angie?*

I thought about how to get more information. If I called the police, they'd want to know who I was and what business did I have with the dead woman. How can I report Angie missing, I'm not a relative or boyfriend or co-worker, I'm just a guy who loves her the way the rain loves the trees.

This is going to take some serious thinking.

I wrapped a towel around my waist, went to the computer, sat down dripping wet and searched through the New York papers' web sites for reports of a dead Jane Doe. There was a short piece about it on the local CBS web site, but it was just a couple of lines that didn't add anything to the report on the radio.

It looked like the only way to settle my worry was to call the police precinct that had jurisdiction over the place where the body was found and try to get a description of the body. The police can pinpoint the name of a cell phone caller in a matter of minutes, so I threw on some clothes and went down to the street. I walked east several blocks until I found a working pay phone, which wasn't easy, pay phones have pretty much gone the way of the dodo bird, with everyone using cell phones. I fed a quarter in the phone and dialed the police station, having copied the number from my phone book at home, and eventually got somebody in missing persons.

A Detective Gisondi sounded bored when I asked him if he could give me any information about the Jane Doe they found that morning out by Floyd Bennett Field. He asked me who I was and why was I asking.

I told him, "Officer, I have a neighbor who hasn't been home in several days, and I was worried this poor dead woman could be her."

He said I had to come down to the station and make out a report. When I told him I was reluctant to get involved, he told me he didn't have time for any bullshit callers who wouldn't follow police policy and procedures. "You could be an instrument of criminal activity," he said. "I give you information, you know what we know, I don't know squat. F'get about it."

Admitting to the officer he had a point, I said, "How about this? I'll email you a photo of my neighbor. You compare it to the dead woman, and I'll call you back. If it is *my* neighbor, I'll come in and make a complete statement."

The officer told me to come to the station or get lost, he wasn't fooling around with some internet freak. Then he hung up.

Now I really had a problem. I needed to know if the dead girl out by Floyd Bennett was my Angie. If it wasn't her, she still could be dead or in hiding or kidnapped or who knows what.

It looked like I had three options. The first was to go to the police precinct and ask to see the dead girl's photo. The detective would insist on knowing my connection with Angie, and I couldn't tell him, they'd think I was some kind of a pervert and lock me up.

The second option was visit Snips, maybe run into Tasha and try to get some information about Angie, which could be tricky, Tasha'd want to know what I was doing nosing around her friend.

The third choice was to hack into the Medical Examiner's database to get a look at a photo of the dead girl found in Brooklyn. But I didn't have the right program to do it. I'd have to call on Kurt, the electrical engineer. He rooms upstairs with Marty and Becka. Kurt told me one time how he and some high school friends hacked into their school guidance office and planted a bunch of impossible college acceptance notices in the programs of the kids with the worst grades. Kurt always says he could get past anybody's firewall. Sure, he was bragging, but the man did have awesome computer skills. It looked like he was my best hope.

Go to the cops, visit Snips and chat up Tasha, or get Kurt to help me do some heavy duty hacking.

It was a no brainer; I went with Kurt.

FOUR

The door to the loft upstairs was unlocked, as usual. Becka was in the kitchen stirring a pot. The air was fragrant with pungent spices. She smiled that angelic smile of hers. I pictured her pregnant—she and Marty talked about having a bunch of kids and feeding them a lot of peaches. John Prine. Becka would look like a fat pregnant Buddha, and Marty would be the lean ascetic monk.

Marty was sweeping up the debris from last night's movie. I asked him if Kurt was home. He told me Kurt was in his room working out and I should go in. "But knock real loud, he's armed and dangerous," he added with that wry grin of his again.

I knocked on Kurt's door and cautiously pushed it open. He was in the middle of his room with a saber in his hand leaping and thrusting at a stuffed doll that was dressed in a banker's pin striped suit and a pig's mask. Kurt greeted me, tapping his fist gently against mine. Kurt's a Jew, but he's into hip hop culture. His hair is this wild curly tangle he calls his Tel Aviv Afro. He had a three day stubble that looked sexy. When I don't shave I look like a bum.

"Have you been in any competitions lately?" I asked, noting the saber in his hand. Kurt said he hadn't competed since college, just practice sessions at the gym.

"Dude," he said. "Did you know fencing is the fastest contact sport in the world? It makes boxing look like fucking tai chi."

"It's not like in the Robin Hood movies, I guess."

"Hell, no. We *never* walk backwards up a staircase." Kurt

took a fencing stance, parried and sank the blade deep into the dummy's chest. "How's the web business these days?" He wiped his face and neck with a towel.

"It's keeping me busy. I'm working on a computer problem. I thought you might, like, steer me in the right direction."

"Sure thing. You need me to help you write some code?"

"It's, uh, kinda not legal."

Kurt's eyes sparkled. Clasping my shoulder with a firm grip, he said. "Just don't ask me to hack into the White House web site. The last guy did that disappeared into the Homeland Security gulag and hasn't been heard from since."

I explained that I was worried about my friend, Angie, who hadn't been home for several days. There was a young woman found dead in Brooklyn over by Floyd Bennett Field and I wanted to make sure it wasn't my friend's body.

"Did you try asking the cops?"

"They wanted me to come down to the station and fill out a report, but I don't think they'd understand my feelings for her. I have a bunch of photos I took from my window..."

"Through your telescope."

"And others I got with a telephoto lens."

"The Brooklyn District Attorney is definitely no art lover. Okay, so whose firewall do you want to breach?"

"The New York City Medical Examiner."

"Cool." Wearing a wolfish grin, he pulled some clothes off a chair and set it in front of his work station. I grabbed another and sat beside him.

"You sure you want to help me with this? It could be dangerous"

"I can send my queries through a bunch of proxy servers, they'll never trace the access request back to me. Plus I have a double helix firewall and a Z-class anonymizer. No program is absolutely impregnable, but mine is about as secure as it gets."

Kurt opened a program that queried computers with password-protected access. When it received a request for a password, it sent arbitrary combinations of letters, numbers and punctuation marks until one was accepted.

"The second program is the killer app," Kurt told me, loading another disc. "It uses heuristic logic to determine what *kind* of password a particular user would most likely select. You feed it a few parameters, like gender, age, occupation, education, and it first tests words that that user is most likely to use."

"Like a fifty year old science major might choose a Star Trek word."

"Exactly."

Kurt soon had the programs loaded and running. He sent the query to the Medical Examiner's central computer, after passing the signal around the world through a dozen intermediaries, keeping his identity and location hidden.

"I need some whiskey!" Kurt said as we both watched the computer submit a series of letter-number combinations. He retrieved a bottle of Bushmils, poured himself a double and offered me a taste, which I declined.

"Too early," I said.

He took a sip and settled placidly into his chair, a smile on his lips. As we both watched the computer screen, all of a sudden the ME database opened right in front of our eyes.

"Hot shit!" Kurt said.

A list of autopsies appeared, with dates, physician name, and status. Some were waiting to be done, some were preliminary reports, others, final. There were three John Doe's and two Jane's.

"Try the Jane Doe from yesterday," I said. "We'll hope they finished the autopsy today."

Kurt selected the file. There was a preliminary report of the physical findings. I read about severe contusions to the face and fractures to the nasal bones, mastoid and the occiput. Kurt explained the mastoid is the jaw bone and the occiput is the back of the head. He's thinking of going to med school. He'll probably invent a device to allow a paralyzed person to walk.

The autopsy report also described cerebral edema and hemorrhage. At the end it listed the cause of death: massive trauma to the face and brain, internal and external bleeding. It was gruesome.

The toxicology results were pending. There were signs of prior trauma to the vagina and anus consistent with repeated sexual assaults. The uterus was scarred, consistent with badly performed abortions.

Kurt moved the cursor over one of the thumbnail photos and was about to click on it when he turned to me. "You ready for this?" he said. "It could be your girl."

I nodded my head, unable to speak. The thought of her body beaten and abused and left for dead made me nauseous. I didn't want him to enlarge the photo, but I *had to* know. I nodded my head and he clicked on the thumbnail.

The image that opened on my screen showed a young woman's battered and bloody face and neck. It had been taken before the body was cleaned and cut open.

The skin was sickly pale, the hair short and copper colored, the cheekbones high. It was hard to tell what the nose looked like originally; it was red and bent to one side.

"It's not Angie," I said, letting out a breath I hadn't realized I was holding. The relief was like a jolt of adrenalin laced with speed. The thought of losing her was such a black hole; such a portent of doom.

"That's good news for you. Right?"

"It is, sure, except . . . "

I leaned closer to the screen and stared at the dead girl's face. Even though it wasn't my Angie, it was still horrible to imagine the blows raining down on her, the girl crying out, the terror in her eyes.

But there was something even more frightening than the image of the bruised and battered dead girl. I turned to Kurt and told him I'd seen the girl before.

"Yeah? When did you see her?"

"Last night. Across the street. At Angie's."

FIVE

While Kurt saved the file with the ME report and the photos of Jane Doe's battered body to a thumbnail drive, he waited for me to explain how come I'd seen the dead girl who was lying in the city morgue only twenty-four hours before. I explained that the woman in the autopsy was named Tasha, that she and Angie used to work together at a hairdresser's named Snips, and that they hung out a couple of times and gone to dinner together and to an art gallery. I told him how I ran into Tasha last night as she was coming out of Angie's apartment.

"Check out her picture," I told him, taking out my cell phone. I scrolled through a photo album with pictures of Angie, some taken from my window, some from the street. It didn't take long to find the ones with her and Tasha. In one photo, shot from outside a restaurant, Tasha was wearing a pink tank top and white shorts. Her dark hair was longer and streaked with silver.

"She changed her hair style," Kurt noted, referring to the images from the autopsy.

"A lot of the girls at the salon change their look all the time. They practice on each other."

"Dude, this is serious shit."

I admitted things were more complicated than I'd first imagined.

I stared at my favorite picture of Angie seated in a café, the sun reflected on her face from the shiny metal table as if posed for a movie scene. Sexy and serene, that was my Angie. Heaven's angel seated at a sidewalk cafe.

What kind of hell had she descended into? The thought that Angie could be in the sort of trouble that got Tasha killed filled me with dread. My gut was knotted up and my foot was tap-tap-tapping the floor with nervous energy.

"Dude, what the hell are you gonna do?" said Kurt.

I said, "I guess I should give these photos of Angie and Tasha to the police. But I really don't want to get involved with them."

"The cops are definitely gonna have trouble with you knowing Tasha is their Jane Doe 'cause you saw the images in the fucking *Medical Examiner's* autopsy report."

We both looked at my favorite photo of Angie. I pointed out that none of my photographs were illegal. I didn't use a hidden camera in a bathroom or a micro lens in my sneakers to look up a girl's dress. It was the same sort of street scenes professional photographers shot every day. Some of them even won Pulitzers for them.

"Do you think they could arrest me for withholding evidence in a murder case?"

"What evidence? All you know is the dead girl visited your friend. You don't know her. You don't know the nature of their relationship."

"True."

"Besides, I *know* you could do as good as the cops accessing your missing friend's records."

I agreed. There are online programs that offer credit checks, reports on recent purchases—even banking transactions and balances. There are search engines that find name occurrences in news media. There were many social media sites where you can mine information if you have the right tools and you pay the companies to share the protected stuff.

I told Kurt I guess I had to give it a shot. But if I didn't come up with anything in a day, maybe two, I'd take what I had to the police. It wouldn't be right, withholding information the police might be able to use to find Angie.

On my way out, Kurt said, “Pete, call me anytime. Anything you need, it’s yours.”

I thanked him and went back to my apartment to start some serious online searches.

The first thing I did was a web search for a phone number for Angelina Andrews. There was no listing for a land-line at her address. Next I used a powerful search program to root out public documents containing her name: high school graduation notices, press reports, filing for applications with the city—there are thousands of databases you can search with a good program.

There were over sixty-five listings in New York for her name. I examined every one, but none of them fit the description of my Angie. That was weird, not finding any public mention of her, since the internet listed our names in thousands of databases that are published online.

I used my E-money account to request a credit check on Angelina Andrews at her current address. The E-money account is a prepaid credit card that I like, it lets me pay in cash. I pay into it with postal money orders and a fictitious name to preserve my privacy. If the rich can hide their financial games in off-shore shelters, why can’t I hide mine in Brooklyn?

The credit check company provided me a detailed summary of her financial state, which was almost nonexistent. She had no saving account, no checking, and no credit card. That was curious, *everybody* has credit cards. She owed several bills, one to a clinic at Kings County Hospital, another to a lab that did medical tests, and one to Con Edison, the electric company.

Even more curious, Angie's credit history seemed to only go back four years. Before that the credit check found no financial records for her. She could have been living with her parents and only operating with cash, lots of people lived that way. Still, it was strange.

She did buy something from an online clothing seller and had it delivered to her job at Snips, but not with a credit card. Probably paid for it with a pre-paid card, like I use. On a hunch, I went to the online seller and found that they sold lists of data about their customers, including birth dates and email addresses. Paying with my E-money account again, I soon had a list of their clients' email addresses. I scrolled thorough the A's, and there was Angie's, right in its proper alphabetical order.

Having someone's email address can get you started on hacking into their computer, it's all in the code imbedded in their email messages. I followed the trail, pinged her address, and soon I was connected to her computer. Her password was a simple one—her name and the year of her birth—so I got past that with no problem.

I checked her Email program's Inbox. It was empty. *Shit.* She must be the type who deletes letters after she reads them. I tried her Sent mail; that was empty, too.

I opened her trash folder, hoping she hadn't thought to empty it: no luck, it was bare. The girl was fastidious to a fault. Or worried somebody would read her mail.

Stumped for the time being, I thought, what the hell, and opened her address book. It had sixteen names and email addresses. Angie hadn't thought to empty that! I printed them out and looked them over. There were four email addresses that went to a Russian email service. *Was Angie Russian?* One of the names in the address book was a Tasha Gordon. That had to be the same Tasha who was in the city morgue.

I had to find Tasha's street address, Angie might be there. I did a quick White Pages check, then a deeper online search, but didn't come up with a street address.

I looked over the document files in Angie's hard drive; they were *all* empty. She had sent them to the trash and then emptied the bin. Why would Angie clear out her hard drive? Unless she wasn't planning on coming back for it. Which *could* mean she knew she was going away.

I used a diagnostic tool to peer deep into her hard drive searching for the old files, but she must have written new files over the old ones and then erased *them,* the data was scattered haphazardly all over her hard drive. It was a serious wipe of the drive.

I studied the bits of data scattered across the drive, all that was left of her deleted files. The data were like paint splatter on a wall, they were disconnected bits of flotsam and jetsam.

Except...

I have a program that searches for repeating words or phrases or even fragments of unusual words on a hard drive. The program filters out common words like *and* or *the,* flagging unusual words, proper nouns, and such. Using the program, I found the proper noun *Hydra* occurring fourteen times on the hard drive, plus twenty instances of fragments of the word. Seven times it was associated with a date. That was interesting.

Several women's names occurred multiple times: Myani, Gladiola, Monsarrate, and Sage. I searched the drive for more pieces; it was like working a psychotic's jigsaw puzzle. I found several instances of *Night* and *Witches.* Even more interesting, I found multiple fragments of those two words, paired. That suggested they belonged together. Was Angie into some sort of pagan cabal?

I was staring at the fragmented data on her computer when my computer screen suddenly went blank. I checked the power strip, but my system was fine, it was hers that was suddenly dead.

Jesus H. Christ. *Somebody just turned off Angie's computer.*

SIX

Right after the image from Angie's computer went blank I grabbed my binoculars and hurried to the window. There was a faint glow in the gap between the curtains of her apartment. A dark figure crossed in front of the light, impossible to tell who.

I watched the entrance to her building. After a few minutes a big guy in a long coat and a pork pie hat came out of the building carrying a satchel. I couldn't see his face in the streetlight. The bag *could* hold a small laptop computer or a tablet, although I didn't know what kind of system Angie used. There was no way to know for certain that he even *was* connected to Angie, his exiting could be a coincidence.

The guy with the satchel stepped into a black Lincoln Town car parked at the hydrant. I focused my binoculars on the car as the driver peeled out, writing the license plate number on the palm of my hand.

Cracking the New York Department of Motor Vehicles would put me smack up against the Homeland Security people. They were *real touchy* about people hacking into their files, and they don't take kindly to whistleblowers revealing all the details of their sordid snooping activities. Those guys are quick to snap the cuffs on somebody snooping around their computers.

I decided to hold off trying to hack the DMV computers. But where was I going to get a line on the creep in the Lincoln?

I looked out at Angie's window wondering what to do next. The street was dark and quiet. Once in a while a car service would pull up and drop somebody off. Most of the car services use Lincoln Town Cars, they're all over New York and they're mostly black. Go figure.

A knock on my door broke my reverie. I looked on my computer screen at the the video feed from the camera I'd mounted in the hall. It showed a small, black and white image in the corner of the screen. Marty's girl Becka and another young woman were standing in the hall. I went to the door and opened it.

"Hi, Pete," said Becka. "I know it's late and all, but you work at night, so I figured it would be okay to drop in on you. I have a friend who needs help with a computer program."

My eyes shifted to Becka's friend. She was a slim young woman with olive skin, long black hair falling to her waist, and piercing black eyes. She smiled at me. Some people smile with their lips and maybe a little of their eyes, but when she smiled her whole face radiated warmth and sweetness. It was the smile of an enchantress.

"This is Jyoti," Becka said. "She joined my yoga class."

I mumbled hello, a little tongue-tied. Becka explained that Jyoti was working for a women's group that needed help with their web site.

"Okay," I said, a little wary, not about the computing, but about the friend. I was more comfortable working alone. But Becka was good to me, so I let them in.

"Becka tells me you're a computer genius," Jyoti said, heading straight to my computer station while Becka held back.

"I just build web sites. It's pretty simple stuff."

"Our site is called Girl Talk," Jyoti said. "It's like a bulletin board with an instant messaging option. We've had a little trouble with some of the messages being vulgar. We don't want to get in trouble with the law."

"The messages are posted in real time," I said.

"Exactly. It'd be great if we could filter them for specific words or phrases, without getting too restrictive."

"I have a program you can use, it's pretty straight forward. I can show you how to filter out select word combinations. It exchanges symbols for the letters so the viewer can imagine what was deleted."

"That sounds perfect!" Jyoti flashed that radiant smile again. She looked at me expectantly, until I realized she was talking about my setting up the program right then and there. I shrugged and pulled an extra chair up to the computer desk.

I opened the filtering program on my computer. Jyoti watched me type in a few expletives in the filter box and FTP them to my own web site. While I worked Becka asked if she could heat up some water for tea.

"I don't normally block any messages, since I just have an email sign-in, but the principle's the same. Try and send me a vulgar message."

Jyoti used her cell phone to send the raunchy email. When I opened my email program, the sentences had different symbols where the banned words had been.

I copied the filtering program to a disk and gave it to Jyoti just as Becka served mugs of tea. They moved to my sofa, sinking into the worn out cushions, I sat in a chair. Jyoti blew over her cup of tea. She had lovely full lips framing a small mouth with perfect, white teeth. Her fingernails were painted a dusky rose. So were her toenails, I could see them through her open sandals.

"You missed a couple of great movies on Friday," Becka said.

I told her work comes first. Jyoti said she was sorry she missed it, she was definitely coming to the next one. Then she asked me what kind of movies I like.

"Quiet ones," I told her.

"Me too," she said. "People hide behind words. It's what they do that counts. Don't you think?"

Becka said, "Without a doubt. Look at Marty. He doesn't go on and on about how much he loves me and can't live without me, but when I need him, he's there, no questions, no excuses."

"My dad was like that," said Jyoti. "On the rare times that he gave you a hug, you knew it was from his heart."

I sipped my tea and thought what it would be like to hug Jyuoti. As much as she looked relaxed in the sofa, she also had a graceful, athletic way about her, as if she could get up on her toes like a ballerina and spin around.

Becka said, "Pete's not loquacious, either, but he's a good listener."

"That's unusual in a man," Jyoti said.

It was probably a compliment, but I didn't say anything. Listening is just something I do, not something I mastered, like Kurt's fencing or Marty's EMT training.

I got up and washed my mug in the sink. Becka brought in the other mugs. Having Becka in the apartment was okay, she was Marty's girl, but Jyoti being here made me edgy. She was so close, and there was no place for me to hide and watch her. I washed and dried the dishes in the sink and put everything away while the girls chatted about the web site.

When they got up to leave, Jyoti saw the telescope in the corner. "Becka told me how you take your telescope up to the roof and look at the stars. Are you searching for alien intelligence?"

I laughed and told her about seeing the international space station. "It crosses the sky in six minutes. You get a better look with binoculars, it's moving so fast."

"Would you show me some time?" she asked.

"Uh, sure. It's a bit cloudy tonight, but the moon will show its face briefly if you're patient, and Saturn's in a good position."

"I'm sorry," Jyoti said, "I promised to meet some friends in the city. Maybe I can I come back another time..."

I told her any clear night, I was usually home, she could knock on my door and I'd take her up to the roof. At the door she shook my hand. Her fingers were slim and warm and strong. I didn't want to let them go.

I watched on my monitor as they walked down the hall, Becka gliding in that smooth way of hers, Jyoti light and rhythmic like a dancer. I wished I'd thought to record her image while she was in my apartment.

SEVEN

After Jyoti and Becka left I worked on the web site of a fisherman who wanted to market his fish nationwide in freezer bags packed with dry ice. It was a cool idea, as long as the delivery service got the fish to the customer before the ice evaporated and the fish spoiled.

I had a little Quick Time video of a big fish on a line fighting fiercely. You clicked on the image of the fisherman and the contest between man and fish played out for you. It was a nice Hemingway moment. I uploaded it to the server, then I grabbed the telescope and headed up to the roof. The door from the stairwell is supposed to be hooked up to an alarm, but it's been disabled as long as I've been in the building.

The clouds had blown out past Coney Island and over the ocean and it was pretty clear, for New York. I sat on a rickety folding deck chair, removed the caps from the big lens and from the eyepiece, and aimed at the ecliptic, the line that the planets follow as they travel across the sky. All the planets orbit the sun along the same plane. It makes it much easier to find the planets in the night sky than if they each circled the sun at a different angle.

Saturn had passed the midpoint and was now in the western segment of the sky. I found her easily enough and adjusted my focus, then switched to a stronger lens. There she lay, a little silver bowler hat set at a jaunty angle, the rings not showing their color bands in my little scope. Still, Saturn was lovely. I looked for her moons, but the sky was too hazy for that fine a viewing. Sitting and looking at her, I felt a deep connection to the ancient star gazers watching the heavens down through the centuries. They didn't have any magnification until Galileo, but they had clearer skies than I did and infinitely more patience.

I heard a cough and saw a flicker of light. Marty had come out for a smoke, Becka doesn't like the smell in their apartment. Luckily, their apartment opens right on the roof.

"Hey," I said, looking his way

He asked what I was looking at. I told him Saturn was in a good position and gave him a look.

"Cool!" he said after watching for several minutes. He looked up at me. "You're like part of an ancient society, aren't you?"

"Kind of, except I don't try to predict the fall of empires."

"You might as well, the whole world's sinking into a superstitious toilet."

He flicked his cigarette over the wall. We watched it arc down to the street, scattering red sparks when it landed.

Marty kept looking down at the street as he said, "Kurt told me you were worried a friend might be in trouble."

"Yeah."

"A woman beaten to death and left out, that's a real sicko." He leaned over the wall and spat. "I haven't found any dead bodies on a call yet, but I've had people die on me on the way to the hospital."

I hated to ask Marty for help, but I didn't see any other way of tracking down the creep outside Angie's building who got into the Lincoln.

"You, uh, work pretty closely with the police, don't you?"

Marty acknowledged he knew a few cops from the local precinct pretty well. I asked him if one of them would track down a license plate for him. He mulled the problem over for maybe ten seconds before telling me he'd done some big favors for a few cops, he was pretty sure they'd do it for him.

I wrote down the license plate number of the guy who

came out of Angie's apartment, telling him it was a black Lincoln Town Car. He promised to give it to a patrolman on his next tour.

Directing the telescope at the crescent moon and focusing the lens, I studied her acne-scarred face while Marty headed back inside. "Let me know you see any alien ships," he said and stepped into his apartment.

I turned my scope to look at Mars, high in the eastern sky. It was too far away to make out the polar ice cap; Mars was just a little blob of hazy color. I pictured myself walking on the surface of the red planet. I'd wanted to go there ever since I was a kid. In my mind I could walk for miles and never run into another soul. It wasn't lonely, either, it was peaceful. I was happy. Eventually I would find a partner to share the experience; a girl with red hair and laughter in her eyes, who sat beside me while I looked through my telescope at the green earth, and who didn't care if she never had anyone else in her life but me.

When I woke up the next day it was early afternoon. I did an internet search for Night Witches, since the words had occurred together in whole or in part so many times on Angie's hard drive. Most of the hits were about witches of different stripes. Vampiresses and dominatrix types. One gal in Vegas had a web site calling herself a night witch pagan earth goddess. She covered a lot of ground.

None of the sites looked like they had any connection to Angie. It seemed weird that she would be involved in some pagan cult, but honestly, how well did I know her? Was she a Christian? An atheist? A Buddhist? I'd never wondered about her spiritual side, just her need to be happy and fulfilled. And loved.

There was one site at the Jewish Museum in Manhattan that had photos from a World War Two squadron of Russian female pilots called the Night Witches. The photos were interesting, but Angie was way too young to have anything to do with them.

Hyrda elicited hundreds of hits; it was a Greek myth, after all. Since there had been dates associated with the word on Angie's computer, I queried for businesses, thinking Angie would have an appointment there. There were several companies using the name: media outlets, a feminist publishing house in Canada, a product for water purification in rural communities, and, bingo, a bar in the Village. I wondered if Josh, Marty's brother, knew it. He tends bar in the Village at the Feral Cat.

I went up and knocked and entered the penthouse. Josh was pouring a mug of coffee in the kitchen. He looked hung over. Bar tending and all the free booze make it easy to get sloshed every night.

"You look tired," I told him, taking the cup he offered me. Thick and strong as an expresso, the brew needed a lot of milk and sugar.

"I hung out and jammed with the band after the club closed last night. We played and drank until the sun came up. It was great, but..." He took a swallow of coffee and waited for the caffeine to reach his brain cells.

I asked Josh if he knew anything about a bar called Hydra.

"Yeah, it's a lesbian hangout on twelfth street in the West Village. Been there forever. Feminists and old lefties hang out there. One night I was in there with a barmaid from my club, we heard these two middle aged women arguing. They sounded like an old married couple. It was cool."

He asked why I wanted to know about the place. I explained I thought a friend of mine was in trouble. "I found the name of the bar on her hard drive."

Josh sipped his coffee. “Isn’t that like reading a girl’s diary?”

I told him I’d never hacked into somebody’s personal computer before, but I really thought she was in trouble and it looked like the only way to get a line on her. I told him Angie’s full name; he promised to ask about her when he went back to work.

My stomach was grumbling, the acids were sloshing around with nothing to dissolve except the lining of my stomach. I went back to my place and heated up a frozen pot pie in the oven. Chicken. A classic. I buy pot pies on sale. Sometimes when they’re on a super sale I get them for two bucks apiece, as many as my freezer will hold. The turkey is good, too. The beef is often chewy and tasteless, but it fills you up. The rare lamb stew on sale is usually excellent, but I’ve never found it for less than two ninety-nine.

The smell of the filling bubbling over onto the bottom of the oven makes me think of my mom and aunt. They cooked gigantic casseroles in the oven so there would be leftovers for the week. We didn’t have a microwave, so a lot of the time the reheating dried up the casserole, but it left the top burned and crispy, which was great. Most people prefer either crunchy or soft types of food. I’m a crunchy type

My mom didn’t have much furniture. A few beds and dressers and a cabinet for liquor; a Formica kitchen table that wobbled, the legs were loose, I guess; and a little television set with a table top antenna you turned and tilted trying to get a decent picture. No carpets. No books or magazines, either, just the TV Guide.

I took the pot pie out of the oven, punctured the crust and watched the steam rise above the table and disappear, like the years of my misspent youth. I thought about some of the other smells I knew growing up. Perfume, of course, they had spray bottles and bottles of bubble bath and such; cigarettes and smoke and overflowing ashtrays; and liquor.

Gin and tonic, my aunt's favorite; rum and Coke, my mom's. She would say it always seemed naked, Coca Cola drunk alone, without any liquor to give it a bite. I never had much of a taste for soda growing up, the corner grocer wouldn't mix it with anything stronger.

I dug into my pie and pulled my mind away from childhood memories, thinking about what to do next. Whenever you start a project—building a web site, say—it's important to have a clear idea of where you're going and what resources you have to work with. You need a *plan.* I decided to look at what I knew so far.

First, what did I know? Angie knew Tasha, and Tasha was dead. Angie could be in the same condition, although I was holding onto the idea she was in hiding somewhere. Tasha had been sexually abused before she was killed, so she may have had a very bad relationship with an abusive partner. It could be a coincidence that she knew Angie and Angie was missing, but I didn't think so.

Second, somebody else wanted to find Angie as well as me. I didn't know how or if the guy who turned off her computer and got into the black Lincoln Town Car was connected to her, but the coincidence was disturbing. I needed to track down the car. If Marty didn't come through with the license plate, I'd have to deal with the information. Somehow.

Third, Angie had a credit history that only went back four years. That could mean she was a new immigrant to the country; she *did* email to people in Russia. Come to think of it, I'd never heard her speak, so I didn't know if she had an accent.

I wondered what she had been doing before she got to New York and started cutting hair. She lived without a credit card or checking account. A low profile lifestyle. Was there something in her past that she was hiding, or somebody she was hiding from?

Fourth, there was her registration for the medical clinic at Kings County Hospital and the bill for tests. I went back over my notes and looked at the dates of the visits. She'd gone to the clinic two years ago, then twice the following year, and four times again this year. Whatever was bothering her must have flared up.

I checked the dates of her visits on my wall calendar. I have the whole year laid out on a big poster calendar over my desk with my deadlines circled in red. I make most of them, too. All her visits were on a Monday. Today was Sunday. On Monday I'd go to the clinic and see what I could find.

Last was Hydra, the lesbian bar in the Village. What would I say if I went there? Who would even talk to me? I hated mixing with people, especially single women, they made me want to hide behind a piece of furniture. If I visited the bar I would have to try and talk to some of them. Maybe my web design stuff could be an ice breaker. It seemed lame.

There was no hiding from Hydra, it was the only lead I had to pursue right now. It was Sunday night, the bar would be open. I couldn't see any other way to move forward.

Hydra, here I come.

EIGHT

I took the subway to West Fourth Street, walked up Greenwich to Twelfth Street and then went west to Eighth Avenue to the club. It was on a corner, with silvery icicle Christmas lights along the awning, even though Christmas was three months away. There was a woman in black leather with a shaved head straddling a Harley talking to another woman outside the club.

I stood outside the bar and curled my toes inside my shoes. Going into a lesbian bar would make me stand out worse than the naked cowboy of Times Square. I like to be anonymous and watch people. No way could I avoid being the object of attention in Hydra. But it might bring me a scrap of information.

I hemmed and hawed and sweated down my flanks, then I gathered up my courage and stepped into the joint. A bar maid saw me come in, frowned, didn't offer me a table. She had a good-sized Adams apple, so it looked like she was a guy underneath. Or used to be. If you find yourself at an early age cast in a role that doesn't fit what's inside, you can come to New York and switch parts. That's maybe the best thing about the city: you can become the person you're meant to be, and nobody accuses you of violating some sacred rule.

A patron asking for a drink called the barmaid 'Ronnie'. I decided not to be so familiar and just addressed her as 'miss.' I got a beer and perched on a stool along the wall, trying to blend in. Across the room a dozen pairs of eyes turned to look at me. I tried to catch snippets of conversation, but the woman on the next stool had her back to me and there was too much chatter to make out what she said to her companion.

There were framed black and white pictures on the wall. One near me showed a woman in a floppy cap and military jacket and pants, holding an old rifle and standing in front of a low stone wall. She had freckles and curly hair. The caption said, *Cumann na mBan.* Scrawled in marker were the words: GUNS & CHIFFON. I wondered what language it was. Portuguese? More likely Gaelic. Judging by the freckles and the low stone wall, she was probably Irish.

Another photo showed a pair of women in flying clothes standing in front of an old World War One biplane. I leaned forward and tried to read the caption, but it was in Cyrillic letters and I couldn't make it out. Russian or Polish, I guessed. Maybe Romanian.

I remembered my Google search of Night Witches and the reference to Russian female pilots. Could this be the same group? I copied down the caption in the photo, not knowing what the Cyrillic letters spelled out. As I formed the last letters, Ronnie the bar maid tapped me on the shoulder.

"The art's not for sale," she told me. She had that look of indifference and disdain you sometimes get in New York restaurants.

"Oh, I'm not interested in buying it. I was just curious what the caption says."

I waited, but Ronnie offered no reply.

"Would these pilots be the famous Night Witches?" I asked her.

"I don't speak Russian," she said and went off.

I turned to face the photo and watched Ronnie in the reflection of the glass. The bar maid went to a table of women in the corner, bent low and spoke into the ear of an older gray-haired women. The woman glanced at me, took out a cell phone and made a call.

I seemed to be an object of interest. Maybe it had nothing to do with Angie. Whatever the truth, there was no one going to spill her story to me, that much was certain.

I took my time finishing my beer. Finally I got up to leave and was half way to the front door when I spotted Jyoti coming in. I froze in place, surprised and delighted to see her.

"Hello, Peter," she said, coming up to me and giving me a hug. The soft press of her body against mine was electric. The memory of her touch remained after she'd stepped back and flashed that diamond smile.

"Hi, Jyoti. Nice place, isn't it?" I winced at the lame comment; I was such an idiot.

"Hydra is cool. I love the atmosphere."

I asked if she wanted a drink; she told me she was meeting some friends and looked around the club. "I don't see them yet. I can sit for a minute."

Ronnie came over with a glass of white wine for Jyoti without being asked. She was a regular. Interesting. I held up my empty glass. The barmaid frowned. "Sure you can handle it?" She returned with another glass, setting it in front of me with a lot of foam layered above the beer.

"I gave you a nice head," Ronnie said and moved down the bar.

"What brings you to Hydra?" she asked. "Are you looking for a date?"

"No, nothing like that." I told her I was looking for a friend of mine. "I haven't seen her for a couple of days. I thought I'd find her here."

"Any luck?"

"No."

"What is her name? Perhaps I know her."

"Angie. Angelina Andrews, to be exact."

Jyoti sipped her drink and ran the name over in her mind.

She said she didn't know anybody in New York by that name. "I met a woman in Italy named Angelicia last year. She's in her fifties." I told Jyoti my friend was a lot younger.

She asked me about my star gazing. I said the weather was cloudy, but the night before I'd had some good viewing. She apologized for not being able to help me with my search, wished me luck and put a ten dollar bill on the bar. I gulped the last of my drink and stood beside her, wishing I could keep her with me longer.

"Don't forget, I'm coming over the next clear night," she said, smiling with her eyes. She walked over to a cluster of women. Most were in their twenties or thirties, but one was the gray-haired woman who had spoken to the barmaid. The younger women were all leaning toward her listening to every word.

Feeling the cloak of loneliness engulf me, I left the bar and stood outside on the sidewalk. A shadowy crescent moon hid behind the cloud cover. It was visible for a few seconds, then swallowed in the gauzy sky, the way Angie was swallowed up by the city.

I descended the subway steps into the harsh light of the tube. The tracks stretched south toward Brooklyn. A long, dark tunnel without a train in sight can be a sorrowful sight. The silence can grab you and bring you down. You imagine the train will never come, like your life will never get on the right track. Like it will never take you to where you really need to be.

I'd known that feeling many a night growing up, sitting in the empty lot across the street from our apartment building, watching men come and go from our apartment building, waiting to be called home. I always had a feeling the future would be bad, and it never disappointed me. My mom got sick and couldn't work. She went downhill fast, lying in bed with chills and fevers, shaking so bad her teeth rattled. I can still hear the *click, click* of her teeth. What was left of them. She was buried in a pauper's grave at the city's expense.

Once you get that sorrowful feeling inside you it's damn near impossible to get rid of it. As I stood in the silent subway station, I had a bad feeling that if I rode all six hundred miles of subway track, I still wouldn't find my Angie.

NINE

An angry alarm jerked me awake, triggering a fear response. I opened my eyes, heart pounding, muscles tensed. I sat up in bed and sniffed the air, fearful the apartment was on fire. It smelled of sweat and despair, like always.

Awake now, I realized it was my alarm clock clobbering my ears. I *never* set my alarm, it's against my religion. I smashed my hand down on the button to silence it and sank back into bed.

Halfway back into slumber land, I suddenly remembered *why* I'd set the alarm: it was to visit the medical clinic at Kings County Hospital that Angie had visited and see could I get some information about her.

After washing up and dressing, I took the No. 2 Train to Kings County Hospital. It's a confusing place; so many buildings, with mixed-up signs out front that seem to lead you in circles. The new building looked promising, so I went in there. An old guard with a bulldog face and a belly hanging over his belt asked what he could do for me.

I told him the clinic I wanted to visit. He looked me up and down as if he was estimating my chance of surviving, then he told me to go outside and down the block to E building. I found the building and the clinic, went to the desk and asked could I register for the clinic.

A young Hispanic girl with dangling earrings and a short pullover that left her midriff bare asked me if I'd been treated at the clinic before. I told her no.

"Every been treated any place else at the County?"

Again, I told her I hadn't. When she learned I had no

health insurance, she shrugged, wrote *SELF PAY* in big red letters at the top of the form, then told me to fill it out.

After filling out the form and giving it back to the girl at the desk, who placed it to the side without looking at it, I sat and watched the people coming and going and waiting. Mostly, they were waiting. Black and Hispanic men and women, many of them young as me, but plenty of older folks, too. There were no magazines or newspapers in the waiting area except for the Watchtower, but there was a raft of brochures about different health issues. Several were about HIV and hepatitis. Pregnancy and birth control.

Three hours later an Indian woman in a colorful flowing dress under a white lab coat came into the waiting room and called my name. She had a stethoscope dangling from her neck and pockets stuffed with paraphernalia. I got up and followed her.

In a tiny cubicle that smelled of oranges, I sat on a plastic chair and looked at the woman. Her name tag said *Gupta, Sreethy, MD.* I wondered if in India Gupta was as common as Smith in the U.S.

She sat on a round stool and read over my history, then looked up at me.

"Mr. Davies, you did not check off any complaints."

"Uh, no. I don't have any."

"Then why have you come to the clinic? Is it to be tested?"

When she said the word tested a light went on in my head. She meant tested for a sexually transmitted disease. An *STD.* Syphillis, say. Or HIV—the devil's door prize. I told her, yes, I'd come in to be tested.

"You also did not fill out the section for sexual partners. It is very important that we know your past liaisons."

"Yeah, I saw that, but, like, I haven't really had a whole lot of relations in a while."

"How long has it been, would you say?" She held her pen

poised over a box, ready to profile me. I was tempted to ask if solitary sex counted, but figured she'd heard that crack a billion times before.

I recalled the last time I'd had a girl up to my apartment. Things had not gone as well as I had hoped. Short fuse, quick explosion. She left without saying good-bye. Just because I wasn't a super stud, she didn't have to walk out like that.

"It's been a year since I slept with somebody."

"I see. Did you use a condom?"

"Yeah." A condom probably wasn't necessary, I was sure I had a low sperm count.

"And before that?" She was writing in my history.

"Maybe six months before that. Could have been a bit longer."

"Have you always practiced safe sex?"

I had to smile at that. Looking through the lens of a telescope or a telephoto lens is about as safe as it gets.

"Pretty much," I told her.

"But not always," she said, jotting down more data on my sheet. "Very well, remove your pants and underwear and put on the disposable gown. I will return shortly."

As she got up to go, I imagined Angie coming in and following the same instructions. In her case, she probably really *did* have reason to worry she'd contracted an STD, the way these guys today fool around and lie about it.

Dr. Gupta came back and had me lie on the examining table. She studied my scrotum first, asking if I had any tenderness. "Do you have pain when you ejaculate?" she asked, gently squeezing my balls.

I assured her I didn't.

She lifted my cock and examined the underside and the opening where I pissed. It was weird having a woman handle my privates, but it was also kind of cool. I started to worry I'd get aroused.

"Have you had any pus or dripping released from the meatus?" she asked, lowering my gown. I told her I hadn't. "Any dribbling or pain on urination?" Again, I denied any problems, relieved to be covered up. I always have sex in the dark.

"I see no signs of sexually transmitted disease. You could be HIV positive, however. HIV does not present with urologic or dermatologic symptoms."

She had me sign a consent to be tested for HIV and asked if I had any questions. I told her I didn't and thanked her.

Wrapping a tourniquet around my upper arm, she swabbed a spot with alcohol, saying, "You may wait in the waiting room for the result if you wish."

When I asked if the results would be held in strict confidentiality, she assured me that they would. That was my cue to find out about their computer system and database.

"I was wondering, doctor," I said as she drew blood from my arm. "What kind of firewalls do you have to protect your data?"

"Excuse me: *firewall?"*

"Yes. That's a program that keeps people from accessing your computer without permission."

"I'm sure we have a very good firewall, but I don't know about any of the specifics. Why do you ask me that?"

"I work with computers, I know how easy it is to break into them. I want to be sure my information is really secure."

Doctor Gupta told me she would ask one of the technicians who was more computer savvy than she to speak to me. I went back to the waiting room. A few minutes later a burly guy in scrubs and red hands came out.

"You the guy wants to know about firewalls?"

I told him I was and gave him my card. He smiled at me. "Nice racket. I thought about getting into web design, but I went for medical tech instead."

"Maybe you could combine them."

"Yeah, that's what I was thinking. Designing web pages for doctors. They're mucho cheapo, though."

I suggested that he check out my web site and email me, I'd be happy to give him some pointers on getting started. Then I asked him about computer security at the clinic.

"Basically, all data is held on a server that's only accessible with a password, plus, you have to have the proprietary software installed on your desktop or the program won't even recognize your request. The I-T people install the programs, so nobody gets access unless they have a professional need to look at the data."

I learned that they used the MediSoft medical software package. It sounded like a simple, meat-and-potatoes application that wouldn't be hard to master. After getting my test results, which were negative, no surprise, I left.

Out on the street, I grabbed a cup of dismal coffee and an empanada from one of the food carts on Clarkson Avenue. The food cart got me thinking about Becka's dream of establishing a healthy fast food business in Brooklyn. I watched the cooks, a chubby Hispanic guy with a shaved head, and a lean, young black woman with dreadlocks. The guy rolled out the dough and filled it with meat and vegetables, the girl threw it in a little oven and served it when it was browned and bubbling. It was a neat, efficient kitchen on wheels.

In my mind I substituted tofu and whole wheat bread for the meat and pastry dough. It could work, I guessed, healthy food was big.

I headed back to my place to see could I download a copy of MediSoft and get into the Kings County database.

I had downloaded a free trial of MediSoft Basic, a stripped down version of their program, saying I was Doctor Nigel Churchill and had a private practice with six other doctors. The program was easy to use, and I was soon setting up databases and diagnostic categories. I used Kurt's software and my anonymous program to interface with the clinic's lab results. When the program asked for a user name, I typed in Doctor Gupta's name. For the password I tried a few variations on her initials, then for the hell of it typed in her first name, Sreethy, which I'd read off her name tag.

The hospital server accepted my identity and opened up its database to me. I was in.

I typed in Angie's name, and soon had all her lab results displayed. The news was as bad as I'd feared: she was HIV positive. But her CD4 count was in the low normal range, according to the normal values the program provided with a right mouse click. That was a relief.

I went to the internet and opened an online website, ASK THE DOCTOR , to learn how they diagnosed an advanced case of HIV. They measured the viral load: the number of viruses in a tiny drop of blood. Angie's numbers were pretty low, 16,000, so her disease wasn't too advanced. I hoped she was taking all the drugs available.

A couple other of her test results had an 'H' by them, which I soon figured out meant 'High.' I checked on the meaning of these values at the same website. Angie's liver enzymes were elevated. Her bilirubin was okay, so the disease wasn't so far along she would be jaundiced and really sick.

Then I looked at the 'differential' applied to persons with elevated liver enzymes. That's the list of diseases that can cause the elevation, especially in the patient with HIV. Cirrhosis was at the top of the list. Liver cancer was right below it. Infections of the liver were there, too.

Now my heart was really sinking. If Angie was hiding somewhere, she was also sick and needed treatment, which meant she needed me to help her more than ever. I *had* to find her, and *fast*. But how? Jyoti didn't know her. Angie's friend Tasha was dead. At her workplace they were cagey as hell.

I had only one lead left: the license plate number on that Lincoln Town Car. If Marty couldn't get the owner from one of his police contacts, there didn't look like any other way to track it down. Hacking into the DMV database was risking serious jail time. I couldn't risk that, the Homeland Defense people could scoop me up and drop me in a hole somewhere.

I climbed the stairs to the penthouse hoping Marty was home and that he'd struck pay dirt.

TEN

When I came into the penthouse Becka was in the kitchen rolling out some dough, Kurt was drawing at an easel by the door to the roof, and Marty was seated on the sofa watching four different sports events on four television sets and playing a video game on a fifth. Marty has satellite TV with five different feeds, so he and his friends can watch games played all over the world. His brother Josh was sitting on the floor leaning against the sofa playing his electric guitar unplugged.

Somebody must have made an impressive play, because Marty switched the game to the big set in the middle and pointed at a player in the instant replay. He got excited and exclaimed about the beauty of the perfect athlete making the perfect goal.

Josh said it was that rare moment when the soul and the body were in perfect harmony. "The best players are ones who meditate and find their soulful heart. That's what gives them the great moves," he said.

Marty said, "That's bullshit. It's genetics and training, it's not some mystical, immortal *soul*. Why do people feel there has to be something more than what's in front of their eyes? You might as well believe in ghosts and alien abductions."

"Man, you just aren't tuned in to the cosmic hum," Josh said. "I hear it in my music. I hear it in my heartbeat. It's everywhere."

"Are you two sure you're brothers?" asked Kurt.

From the kitchen Becka said, "Brothers who are close in age have to differentiate early on to establish their identities."

"What's your opinion, Pete?" said Marty. "Which one do you go with —Rod Serling or Albert Einstein?"

"I agree with Marty that the supernatural is an outdated fiction. But that doesn't mean you have to give up a belief in the sublime. Like a perfect love. Or a moment of pure bliss."

"Love is chemistry," said Marty. "Romanticism is another escape into fantasy."

"Love is the only antidote for loneliness," said Josh. "*And* despair."

I went over to where Kurt was working at his easel. He was sketching something in pencil. I asked him what it was.

"Dude, it's the latest iteration of Kurt World. It's, see, this monster playground for little kids. It challenges their intellect and it's safe at the same time. Check it out."

He showed me a jungle gym composed of interlinking clear Plexiglas cubes. A child went in one end and could climb to all sorts of heights, look out at his parents, even end up on the other side of the playground, and there were hatches where a parent could scoop out a child that was lost.

"And if the kid gets lost and scared, every fourth cube has an escape hatch the mom can unlatch and pull her child out."

It was the most amazing structure I'd ever seen. Next he showed me a merry-go-round that the children propelled with their legs.

"See, it uses the same mechanism as a bike so the pedal is freewheeling, it won't smack your legs when you stop pedaling. The kids don't need their parents to push them, they're under their own power!"

It was magical, and I told Kurt he had to build one.

"I've applied to a couple of competitions for grants and stuff. I'm waiting to hear from one in Baltimore and another in Portland. Portland's my best shot."

Kurt asked me how I was doing with my search for Angie.

I told him things didn't look very good; she'd been sick, and she could be in a hospital somewhere. I didn't say what the problem was.

Marty pumped his arm in the air over somebody's goal. Calming down, he reached into his shirt pocket and took out a slip of paper. "I got the address on that car you were asking about. It's owned by an escort service. Does your friend work for them, 'cause if she does, my brother needs a date."

Josh answered Marty with a rush of chords ending in a choking blues note.

I took the paper from Marty and read it. *Yummy Escort service.* The name gave me a renewed sense of dread. Could Angie have moonlighted for a place like that? It would explain how she got infected with HIV, her 'date' probably didn't use a condom. Maybe she kept it professional and just hung on the arm of some up-scale professional type, but I feared the worst.

The thought of Angie letting greasy guys paw her body made me nauseous. And angry. I hated those sleazy bastards, with their cash in one hand and their dicks in the other. It was just another form of rape.

I thanked Marty and went down to my apartment. I didn't want to look for the escort service on the Internet, it was too upsetting. I thought I'd close my eyes just to shut out all the thoughts scrambling around in my brain, but that only loosened my imagination. Images of Angie in a stretch limo with some rich guy pulling down her panties spun through my mind like planets jerked from their orbits.

I thought I would go crazy. Eyes open or closed, I couldn't get the dark images out of my mind. Thinking I would never sleep again, I pulled a blanket up over my face, stared up into the darkness, and fell asleep.

When I opened my eyes it was dark outside the window. The clock read three-thirty. I'd slept half the night. Weird. I made a cup of instant coffee, washed my face with cold water, sat down at the computer. It was now or never. I typed in *Yummy Escort Service* and hit the search button. The company was located in lower Manhattan, not too far from the Ground Zero site. It had a web site that promised provocative, fun partners for New York affairs. *Laughs and loving looks. The girl of your dreams hanging on your arm and your every word. All major credit cards accepted,* the ad promised. There was a statement in bold letters with exclamations points warning that escorts were for casual company only. Yeah, right.

There were also thumbnail photos of the escorts, along with "personality profiles." Supposedly some were quiet, demure, sweet; others were chatty, perky, lively. All the women were great dancers and fabulous lookers. There were no photos of Angie or Tasha.

The site invited customers to type in their credit card number for a *guaranteed perfect date*. Sure. Give them your card and in sixty seconds it will be sent to a criminal organization in Bulgaria or Russia and they'll use it for cash and purchases.

I didn't like the fact that Angie might have been mixed up with this sordid stuff, but there it was. No point denying it. There was only one thing to do if I was ever going to find Angie.

Visit Yummy Escort Service.

ELEVEN

At noon I stepped into a coffee shop across from the Yummy Escort Service. I figured if the place was a brothel they would be doing a bang-up lunch trade. Inside the coffee shop there was a wooden lattice divider that separated the sit-down trade from the lunch counter denizens. I found a seat behind the divider, which had photos in little ornate frames. One of the best ways to watch someone is to place your eyes behind a fence or screen. From a distance they see the screen; from my vantage site, I could see the building clearly.

I sipped a cup of tea and watched. A couple of young guys approached the door and rang the bell. One guy had a diamond earring in his left ear, a short, spiky haircut and walked with a rolling sailor's gait. I wondered if it was from laboring at sea or overdoing it on the dance floor. The other guy was beefy and solid and didn't swing his arms as he walked. When he stood in front of the door he tucked his thumbs in his belt, cowboy style.

A burly fellow with lidded eyes, a barrel chest and the arms and neck of a weight lifter answered the door. Weight lifter exchanged a few words with the lads and let them in.

A police car cruised by, slowed as it passed the building and drove on. I read the logo on the side: *to serve and protect.* I guessed they knew about the service. Maybe they were watching it, like me.

As I sipped my tea and looked through the slats in the divider, a Lincoln Town Car pulled up in front of the building. The license number was the same as the one that pulled away from Angie's apartment the night her computer went blank. Two girls, dark and Asian looking, from Thailand, maybe, came out accompanied by an older woman. Recruits? The older woman, also Asian but light skinned and heavily made up, led them to the entrance. The burly doorman opened the door and stepped aside as the older woman led the girls inside. The door closed behind them like a prison gate.

A sickly feeling churned up my insides. It was the kind of feeling I had when I was a kid and the cops slapped my mom and my aunt around. It happened when I was maybe ten, before my mom got sick. Two big cops came in and tore up the place; I never did understand what they were so pissed about. They knocked both the women around pretty good and left. No arrest and no explanation.

I didn't have to play outside for almost a week after that, they were too beaten up to go out and hustle up any men. I felt sad and helpless and angry and scared all at the same time. When we ran out of food, not even pasta and butter, they got dressed up, put on their makeup and sprayed themselves with perfume, and went back to work.

Watching the young girls being hustled into the Yummy Escort Service, my gut told me to head for the subway and go home; give up this foolish idea of finding Angie and *saving* her. Just connect with the internet and cruise cyberspace. I could go back to reading the blogs of lonely people. The honesty and raw emotion that people pour into their web sites is incredible; it can be more honest and real than conversations between two people seated across from each other slinging bull shit. Liberating anonymity.

Though it was tempting to split, I *had* to know what happened to Angie. I owed it to her. I owed it to myself. I had to go into the service, there was no other way.

I rang the bell out front and greeted the big bruiser at the door. He had bad teeth, bad breath, and bad manners. He looked me up and down as if measuring me for a suit to wear at my funeral. “Whaddya want,” he said. It was more a statement than a question.

I told him I'd visited his web site, which was very professionally done, and I wanted to hire an escort for a concert.

“You paying by credit card?” he asked.

I told him if that was the recommended method, yes, I would use plastic.

He opened the door just wide enough for me to squeeze through, then he slammed it shut and led me down a hallway to a small waiting room. It was dimly lit. There were men's magazines on a black lacquered table. A sexy rhythm and blues song was coming from speakers on the floor. On a table in a covered aquarium was a snake. It was maybe three feet long. I went over and looked at it. The snake moved toward me and put out its tongue. I wondered if it could smell me through the air holes in the top.

The same older Asian woman who had led the girls out of the car came into the room carrying a photo album. She wore a black dress, black stockings and black pearls. The pearls aren't exactly black, they're more a gun metal grey. I thought they would look better against a white dress, but she seemed to be into a Johnny Cash look.

She smiled when she saw I was looking at the snake. “They are beautiful creatures, are they not?” she said, stepping to the tank. She began to lift the lid. “Would you like to hold her?”

I took a step back even though I figured she wouldn't hand me a poisonous snake that could bite me. After all, she *was* a business woman, and biting the hand that pays you is deadly for a business.

“Uh, that's okay, I'm sure it's a fine pet.”

She reached her hand into the tank. The snake slithered

up and wrapped itself around her wrist and lower arm.

"You see how she loves to hug me? Snakes are affectionate creatures. And loyal."

She unwrapped the snake, returned it to the aquarium and replaced the lid.

"I am Pearl," she said and pointed to the love seat. We sat down together.

As she smiled at me I noticed that her teeth were perfect and brilliantly white. It looked like every one of them had been capped.

Pearl asked if I'd ever used their service before. I told her no, I hadn't. She said that in addition to providing escorts for social events, they also had "companionable" women available on line to talk to and "share confidences."

I told her I preferred going out on a date with a real woman. There was a concert I wanted to attend Friday night, but didn't want to go alone.

This seemed to encourage her. She asked for some identification and my credit card. I gave her my credit card and my library card. Seeing the library card, she asked didn't I have a driver's license. I explained that I didn't drive, I was a New Yorker.

"You have no photo identification of any kind?" she asked.

When I pulled out my wallet and thumbed though it, the Madam leaned over and looked closely at it. Maybe she was looking for signs that I was a cop.

"What is that card?" she asked, poking a finger into my wallet.

"My business card," I said. "It doesn't have a photo on it."

In the blink of an eye her hand darted to my wallet and plucked out the card. She must have been a great pickpocket. She tucked the card into the photo album, saying, "Tell me what type of woman do you want for a companion: Caucasian. Asian. Black. Hispanic?"

Remembering Angie's emails to Russia, I told her that I thought Russian women with a thick accent were very sexy. "I grew up on James Bond spy stuff," I told her.

"Russian girls are very chic," she told me with a wink, opening the album and thumbing through it. The women were dressed in revealing outfits, showing a lot of cleavage, pouting and looking directly into the camera as if promising something special.

Thinking a younger woman might be newer to the business and perhaps more open, I pointed to a girl who looked about seventeen.

"Svetlana. A wonderful girl. She has a great sense of humor. You will get along with her very well." She paused, put a finger to her lips as if considering something. "You said you wanted a girl for a concert on Friday this week?"

I confirmed that was my intention.

"I believe that Svetlana is here. If you wish you may spend time with her now in a quiet, private setting." She leaned closer, letting me feel her body. "We have soft music and champagne. You could dance, drink, laugh—whatever your heart desires. Svetlana wants you to like her."

I told her now would be fine. She stood up and led me through a door. We went down a narrow, dark corridor. At the last door Pearl knocked three times, opened it, ushered me in.

"Svetlana, this is Mister Peter Davies. You will be his true companion." Pearl winked at me again and shut the door behind her.

I looked at the girl. She was sitting on one of those narrow half-coaches they call an opium bed you're supposed to half recline on and smoke a hookah. She had wide hips, thick legs, and a short black leather skirt. The zipper on her leather top was open half way down, promising a festival of flesh.

The girl held out a hand. I wasn't sure if I was supposed to shake it or kiss it. I squeezed her fingers and sat on the end of the little bed.

"How do you do?" she asked in a flat American accent. Maybe she learned English watching *My Fair Lady.* "I am Svetlana." She gave her name a little Russian accent, losing the English flair for a moment.

"I'm Peter. That's Petrov in Russian, isn't it?"

"Vury good. You speak Russian?"

"No, just a few words. How long have you been in New York?"

Svetlana looked down at her lap without answering. After a moment, she looked up, her eyes not quite as playful. "I am here for you. Let me make you happy."

When she reached for my shirt and began to unbutton it, I got this uncomfortable feeling. It wasn't that she wasn't pretty and sexy; she was. It's just I didn't have any intention of having sex with her.

I took her hands in mine and said, "Svetlana, could we like sit together for a little and snuggle?"

She looked into my eyes as if she saw into the locked diary of my soul.

"Uff course, Petrov. Take as much time as you want. You are the boss. I am your slave of love."

She got up, went to a CD player and put on some soft jazz. Then she held out her hand to me. I got up, took her in my arms and began dancing. Her perfume was flowery and sweet. Svetlana kissed my neck and laid her face on my chest. She pressed he soft body against me and gently pushed her hips into me.

I wrapped my arms around her and swayed with the music. Her body was distracting me from my purpose. I told myself to stay clear-headed and stick to my plan.

After swaying to the music for awhile, she reached down to my crotch and stroked me. I took her hand away.

"Don't you like me?" she asked, pulling her face back from my chest.

"You are very pretty."

"You can do what you like with me. You understand? Whut ever you like."

"I understand. It's just that, I've got something troubling me." She looked up to my face, puzzled. "It's not about you."

"Your heart is heavy," she said. "I feel it when you come in." She stroked my hair and kissed my chest. "Tell Svetlana what is your trouble. Svetlana understands."

I kissed the top of her head and stopped swaying.

"My friend has disappeared. One day she was just, gone. I need to know she's okay."

"You wurry for your friend."

"That's right. I think she might have worked here for a while. Angie Andrews?"

At the mention of Angie's name Svetlana'a body stiffened. She pulled away from me, not letting go, but opening a gap between us. We danced stiffly for another few minutes. Finally she said, "Nobody I know that name."

I tried to look into her face but she avoided my eyes. After dancing a bit more, I whispered in her ear, "It's really important to me Svetlana. I love her."

Svetlana wouldn't speak or look at me. She continued dancing stiffly, her body now a foreign shore. I didn't know what else to say to her. It looked like the visit to the brothel was a bust.

"Maybe I better go," I said.

"Petrov," she said softly. She looked up at me with fear in her eyes. In a whisper she said, "I am supposed to give you pleasure. If I do not, Miss Pearl, she will be angry. She will punish me."

I looked over her shoulder at the small round mirror on the wall. No doubt it concealed a video camera. The Madam was probably watching, making sure none of the men made a date with the girls. They probably used the film to blackmail the clients, too.

"Please, Petrov, let me pleasure you."

I felt a powerful wave of affection for Svetlana, seeing her so vulnerable and in danger. It was up to me to protect her from the wolves.

I brought my lips close to her ear and said, "You pretend to give me oral sex, I'll pretend to get off."

We turned so that my back was to the camera. Svetlana got down on her knees, opened my trousers and took my cock in her fingers. She stroked me as gently as she would stroke a newborn baby.

I bent my head back as if I were enjoying waves of delight and tried to make sexy sounds. The funny thing was, as I thought about saving Svetlana from punishment, I started to become aroused. She looked up at me, surprised, then she smiled and continued her gentle ministrations.

But when Angie came back into my thoughts, my desire left me. Still, I moaned as if enjoying a terrific climax just to satisfy the watchers. Svetlana closed up my pants and got to her feet. I hugged her for a long moment. The way she clung to me, I could feel her gratitude. It looked like I'd saved her from a beating.

I kissed her gently one more time and started to release her when she brought her lips to my ear and whispered, "Bad girls are rusalka."

Svetlana abruptly pulled away, turned and left the room without looking back.

Confused, I went back to the lobby. Pearl was there, smiling. Probably watched the whole thing on a video camera. She asked what time should Svetlana be at my apartment. I said eight o'clock and started to give her the address when she held up my business card.

"We have your address, Mister Davies. Svetlana will be there promptly at seven."

She didn't offer me a receipt for the time I would be billed, but I didn't want to engage her in a conversation, so I left.

Outside, I walked slowly along the block, not paying attention to where I was going. Svetlana's message was crashing around in my head: *"Bad girls are rusalka."* What did that mean? Was she dead? Was she deported? Married? I had to get to the internet, call up a Russian-English dictionary, and find out what the hell she was talking about.

TWELVE

Back in my apartment I went on line and found a free translation service, Tower of Babel. I typed in *rusalka;* the translation came up with one word: *mermaid.* There were no other options listed. No mistake. No ambiguity. *Mermaid . . . Bad girls are mermaid.* What did that mean?

It sure didn't mean that Angie was starring in an Off-Broadway musical. It sounded like the girls in the escort service all ended up in the ocean feeding the fish and crabs and anything that ate flesh.

Thoughts in my head scattered themselves like a fragmented hard drive. *Angie a mermaid?* But *why?* Even supposing that she *had* worked for the escort service, what reason could they have for *killing* her? If you steal from your pimp, he beats you up or withholds your drugs. You don't destroy your meal ticket.

Picking up my favorite photo of her, one in a gold-colored frame, I looked into her eyes, trying to believe that Svetlana had been lying. Or mistaken. Or that she meant something different. Maybe I heard it wrong. I scrolled through the Russian dictionary looking for words that sounded like *rusalka* but were a little different. Nothing sounded close.

There was no point kidding myself, Svetlana was talking about cement overshoes. I'd been stupid, stupid, stupid thinking Angie would escape the fate that Tasha suffered. What other explanation was there for her disappearing the way she did? The plants on her windowsill were shriveling up and dying; her body was bloated and decaying somewhere in the Atlantic. It was too horrible to imagine; too logical to doubt.

I took a red felt marker and wrote the word *rusalka* on the glass, right over her face. It was childish, I know, but so what? It was my picture. My Angie.

I went up to the roof without the telescope. Mars was high in the southeastern sky, an unblinking light set in a deep purple sea. There was no “music of the spheres;” space was a vast emptiness. It was cold and airless. If I could build a ship and wander in the soundless stretches between the stars, I’d be right at home. It would be even better than walking on Mars.

In space I could empty my mind of memories. Defrag my brain. Become as silent and indifferent as the frozen rocks wandering out there. There would be no sunrise or sunset to mark the days. Time would slow and stop.

Best of all, there would be no one to see me. No one to get a glimpse of the ugly person inside and turn away in disgust. That would be beautiful. That would be freedom. Wandering in space, I would be free.

I went downstairs to sleep just as the pink tongue of the morning licked the ear of the sky. I closed the curtains, turned the ringer off my cell phone, and fell into bed without taking off my clothes.

I woke up wrapped in my blanket so tight, I felt trapped until I realized where I was and what had happened. Uncoiling the blanket, I saw on the alarm clock it was six in the morning—a time of day unfit for human consciousness. I stumbled to the bathroom to take a leak and was startled at the face in the mirror. The pale, pasty mug looked like somebody in prison. It reminded me of the years I spent in Juvie Hall.

Two years, eight months for assault. My foster mother's boyfriend was beating on one of the girls. Doing other things to her and beating her to keep the girl from telling, I was sure, though she never said and I never saw it. But when I heard her crying and found him slapping her around in a dark little closet of a room with a mattress on the floor, I took my knife and stuck him in the kidney. Kidney's are a great place to stick somebody, the organ bleeds internally like a son of a bitch, and the pain is excruciating.

The foster mom had me arrested, and the girl being beat was afraid to dime on the boyfriend. But I was lucky; my lawyer subpoenaed the girl's medical records. They showed evidence of sexual abuse, and the judge put two and two together, even without the girl's testimony, so he gave me the minimum sentence.

Juvenile Detention. Bad food, bad air, bad ass guards. You show any weakness or express any need, they turn it against you and you're pinned in a corner with nowhere to turn. Want something? Don't ask, they'll make you pay ten-fold to have it, and then withhold it from you in the end, just to put the screws on you. To cement the power they have over you.

That's the essence of imprisonment: making you feel powerless. Totally dependent on the arbitrary decisions of a moron who can put you in solitary and beat the crap out of you. Who *enjoys* it. Who gets *paid* to inflict pain and humiliation.

I splashed cold water on my face, trying to wash away the memories. I changed my clothes, dropped the dirty ones on the floor in my closet, and went to make some coffee. I found the milk was sour and I was out of instant coffee. On the way out of the lobby I ran into Josh with his guitar, coming home from an all night gig.

"Yo, Pete, my man; how ya been?" He looked me up and down. "You look like shit, bro," he said. "You all right?"

"I've had a cold."

"Looks more like the plague.'" Josh pulled the guitar strap off his shoulder and set the instrument down. He was a tall, good-looking fellow with a scruffy beard and an Irish cap set back on his head. "You didn't find your girl, I guess."

I shrugged. The words stuck in my throat.

"You *did* find her and she turned you down?" he asked.

"I think she's dead, like her girlfriend." When Josh asked what happened I said I couldn't talk about it right then.

"That's cool, I understand." Another resident came out of the elevator. Josh hoisted his guitar and stepped toward it. "You coming back soon?"

I told him I was just going for milk and coffee.

"I got something for the coffee," he said," adding as the elevator door was closing, "It'll knock out that cold!"

A while later I was sitting at the computer drinking coffee and watching the screen saver march across the screen over and over again when I heard a knock on the door. I went to the computer and saw Josh in the video camera holding up a bottle of liquor. He held it close to the camera so I could read the label: Jameson. I let him in.

Josh opened the bottle of Jameson, explaining it was his pay from playing at the bar. He poured a healthy dose of whiskey into my coffee and a double for himself, which he sipped. "This is the best fucking treatment for the flu. Trust me, I know what I'm talking about."

I tasted the coffee. It was greatly improved, no doubt about that. A few more sips and the ache in my heart and the firecrackers in my head eased a little.

"Nothing like a shot of Jameson to make the bitter taste sweet. Eh?" said Josh.

I didn't answer him. Words. Conversations. They were just distractions that deflected you from the reality all around you.

"We're all in solitary confinement," I told him.

"Yeah, that's true, but you can still beat your tin cup on the bars and get a response."

We sipped our drinks in silence for a time. Finally Josh said, "Your girl's dead. It's a bummer. Granted. But you still gotta keep on truckin'. Still got to face the dawn, you know what I'm sayin'?"

I didn't know and didn't care. Josh mixed another round and we drank some more.

"We're showing a couple of great indie films on Friday. Why don't you come watch them with us?"

I told him I was never leaving my apartment again.

"What you gonna do for food?

"I'm going on a hunger strike."

"Yeah, but you still need to go out. You got to do your laundry."

"I'll live in my bathrobe."

"Cool. You could stand in the window and flash people across the street."

"I'm never lifting the shades."

"*Man,* you're in some serious funk. Better drink up."

As we sipped the second drink Josh looked around the room, saw the photo of Angie with the word *rusalka* written with red marker across the glass.

"What's that, her nickname?" he asked, pointing at the photo.

"It's Russian for mermaid. I got a tip that she could be something like that."

"*Damn,* no wonder you're fucked up." He sipped his drink and looked at the picture some more. "You're sure it's not something to do with the Mermaid Parade down at Coney Island?"

"I don't think so."

"Yeah, that would be too easy."

Josh stayed until the bottle was half empty. When he left he promised to look in on me the next day.

I sat at my kitchen table feeling like a fish that had been filleted. Why did I have to fall in love with a prostitute? I was an idiot living in a dream world. Now the dream world was shattered. I wanted to take the shards and rip open my skin, pull out my liver and kidneys and heart and throw them off the roof.

I decided to let the cops handle the whole mess. That's what we paid taxes for—right? Let them find out what happened to Angie and who did what.

I found the number for Detective Gisondi and struggled to enter the numbers on the phone, but my eyes were bleary and my hands were sluggish. Each time I tapped one of the numbers, it felt like I was using somebody else's hand. That was totally weird.

After a single ring I heard a gruff voice say, "Gisondi. Missing Persons." I felt a powerful urge to hang up the phone, but I realized even though caller ID would be displaying *Unknown Number*, he'd probably still have the ability to trace the call back to me in the end.

I opened my mouth, but the words stuck in my throat. Gisondi said, "You got a voice or you just want me to hear you breathing?"

"Oh, sorry," I said. "I spoke to you last Saturday about a friend of mine I was worried about. I thought she was the girl they found down by Floyd Bennett field."

"You're the wise guy wouldn't come in file a report."

"That's right. Well, I found out it wasn't my friend's body, but I still think she's dead."

"Oh? What makes you think so?"

"Because she's disappeared. I think she was thrown in the ocean. With weights so she'd sink. That's my best guess, anyway."

"You *guess,"* Gisondi said, "Are you on drugs or something? Your voice sounds fucked up."

"No, I'm not on drugs, I've just had a few drinks. But see, *her* friend *was* killed and you need to know who she is."

"Look. Mac. Give me your name and address and I'll send a patrolman around to take your statement."

"Um, I think I should remain anonymous."

"Not that crap again."

"Hey, you take anonymous tips all the time, right? You've got the signs on the sides of the buses. It's police policy. It's accepted."

"We take statements from people who want to report crimes, not drunks who *guess* their girlfriend has been lost at sea."

"Okay, I'm guessing on that part, but I *do* know the name of the Jane Doe that was found in Brooklyn by the old airfield. It's Tasha. I have her picture, she used to work with *my* friend at a hairdresser's."

"Tasha who?"

"Gordon. Tasha Gordon. She works at a place called Snips."

"And just how do you know this Miss Gordon?"

Explaining I wanted to help the police but still stay anonymous, I offered to email him the picture and the address where they worked. He could get more information from the boss.

Gisondi covered the mouthpiece and spoke to somebody else; I couldn't make out what he said. Finally he agreed. He gave me his email address. I promised to send the stuff right out to him.

I said, "You can email back to me when you find her killers. How's that?"

"Pal, I'm not sending you squat until you identify yourself," he said and hung up. Gisondi probably figured he'd be able to identify me from my email. He didn't know I kept an anonymous account that was pretty much untraceable.

I went to my computer, opened a program that sends messages by way of a half dozen proxy servers, and sent the detective photos of Angie and Tasha together. I also sent him Angie's home address, the name of the place she worked, Artistry, and the name of the escort service. I wanted nothing more to do with Angie and the creeps who killed her. I only wanted to turn my mind into a whiskey-soaked mass and stop thinking altogether.

When I was finished with the email I went out for a walk. Walking in the city is kind of like walking on Mars. As long as you stay a stranger, all the living who pass you don't notice, so you may as well be alone.

THIRTEEN

I walked north through busy streets. Sidewalks were spilling over with vendors selling fruits and vegetables, cheap household goods, tacky furniture and gaudy clothing. Always a young man sat on a high stool watching over the goods, keeping thieves at bay.

A bus stopped and kneeled, letting an old woman step up and in, then it pumped up its hydraulics, leveled out and pulled away from the curb. You have to admit, the city provided a lot of services. The exhaust didn't even smell: natural gas engine. What a city.

I walked on until I reached the Brooklyn Bridge. The broad entranceway funneled cars along big, looping ramps. The cars on the ramps were stopped. A few leaned on their horns. I remembered a cartoon from an old Mad Magazine I picked up in a used books and magazine store. The cartoon showed the Long Island Expressway with miles of cars at a dead stop, drivers leaning out their windows. In the distance a giant asphalt machine was laying a new road directly on top of the cars and people, burying them, the way ancient Roman streets were buried by centuries of garbage.

New Yorkers would never accept such a drastic measure. Too many special interest groups.

I followed the pedestrian walkway up onto the bridge, trying not to think about jumping. There are spiked barriers at the entrances that make it near impossible to climb out onto the edge, but the ones who are determined find a way to get past them. There was a steady stream of skaters, bikers, joggers and straggling pedestrians. I breathed the fragrant fumes of the idling cars below me on the bridge.

Half-way across the bridge, I stopped and watched a cargo ship heading out of the greater New York harbor. Maybe it was bound for Africa. Or Europe. The life of an able bodied seaman came to mind. I imagined myself walking bent over through the restricted passageways deep in the bowels of the ship, the throb of the great diesel engines humming through the floor plates. I saw myself on deck holding onto the railing and working with thick ropes, a pounding rain freezing my fingers and making the deck slick and dangerous, while waves broke over the bow and the ship bobbed and heaved in the swells. It sounded like a life that kept you occupied, so you didn't think too much about what you left behind on the shore.

My hand on the bridge railing seemed to be sticking to the metal surface. I drew it back and looked, but there was nothing sticky on the metal. My hands felt heavy and swollen, though they looked like they always do. It was that creepy feeling again like they were somebody else's hands.

My skin has always been ugly to me. I have a sense that I have alligator skin covered with warts and boils and giving off the stench of a swamp. It's not really true, I know. Aside from a few acne scars and a long white line from a knife down my flank, my skin is the normal pale, colorless, boring European skin that belongs in an ice bound village somewhere in Finland.

I watched two young women walk by with jaunty steps and cheery banter. They were smiling and nodding and swinging their arms with vigor. They were in high spirits. It was depressing how light-hearted they seemed. Didn't they know despair was the foundation of all thought, and death is the answer to the last question you'll ever ask?

I headed back toward Brooklyn, letting the merry women go on ahead. There was nothing to eat in the apartment, my frozen pot pies were all gone, so I picked up a couple of slices of white pizza and a cold beer and took them home. I stopped a half block from the apartment building and looked over the street. There were cars parked on both sides, even in front of the hydrant. No Lincoln Town car. No bull-necked thug in a cheap suit loitering near the entrance. Still, he could be waiting for me on the stairwell.

Paranoia is a survival mechanism. I entered my building, took the elevator up to my floor, and got into the apartment without any problems. The heavy lock rotating and sliding into place gave me a secure feeling. I sat in the kitchen to eat dinner. The pizza was cold, the beer was warm, and I was out of hope.

FOURTEEN

I was lying in bed watching a movie on my tablet with the sound off. I like to make up stories about the characters on the screen, the story lines they put out are so predictable, they drive me nuts. In my mind the cute girl sitting on the sofa talking with an older woman was discussing becoming a surrogate mother for a paralyzed woman in an iron lung. The girl was having second thoughts. The mom was telling her, "dear, the surrogate mother thing would be *such* a boost for your plans to become a famous actress, all the big stars are traveling the world contributing to poverty and disease."

I liked that line, "contributing to poverty and disease." The bimbo mom meant they were making a contribution to *end* social ills, but I had her doing a malaprop kind of thing.

A rap at the door interrupted my imaginary dialogue. I wished the rapping had come from the television, I didn't want any company.

I heard Kurt's voice saying, "Yo, Pete! You gotta come see this!"

I looked at the clock on the computer screen. Three o'clock. Was it afternoon or middle of the night? The light scorching the curtains told me afternoon. What day was it? It was Friday, according to the big calendar on the wall. With the whole year laid in one big display, it's supposed to get me organized and make me fulfill my contracts on time. Yeah, right.

I got up and went to the door. Kurt was standing there dressed in army surplus fatigues, which was goofy since he'd never been in the military and hated everything it stood for.

He had a big smile on his thick lips. Girls must love kissing him. And that riot of curly hair probably drives them nuts. Some guys have all the luck.

"What's goin' on?" I asked him.

"Dude, Marty and I finished building the McVeggie Cart for Becka. It's up in the penthouse. You gotta come see it."

I told him I didn't feel like going out. He looked me up and down, saying, "Looks like you haven't washed in a month. But hey, we're not snobs, we'll take you the way you are. Come on, put some clothes on."

When I again declined his offer his eyes got soft and serious. "My friend, you've been hiding in your pad too long. It's time you got out and interacted. Join the living."

They were good friends who'd helped me many a time. The least I could do was go up and see their engineering work.

"Let me brush my teeth and take a leak, I'll be up."

"Okay. I'll have a pot of coffee on, you look like you need it."

He wasn't wrong. In the bathroom mirror I found a puffy eyes, matted hair, filmy teeth and clothes that a homeless guy would be ashamed of. I splashed some cold water on my face, brushed my teeth, and found some half-way fresh clothes piled on the floor that didn't smell. Much.

Upstairs Becka was in the kitchen feeding baking trays into the oven. On the counter she had little pastries drying on a wire rack.

"You got the permit. Eh?" I said.

"Not *exactly*," said Becka, her face turning forlorn.

Marty explained that he and Kurt had hacked into the DCA Licensing Center and downloaded a copy of a vendor's permit. "It was really approved for a guy in Queens. We used Photo Shop to change the name on the permit and printed it out."

"I spilled some tomato sauce on it to make it look authentic," said Kurt. "We had it laminated so nobody could examine the paper. Pretty slick. Huh?"

I agreed they were indeed very slick. Becka still had doubts about going out without a real permit.

"The permit *is* real," Marty said. "It's just not *yours*."

I sniffed the air. "What're you cooking? It smells nutty."

"Cashews, corn and yogurt cheese in a brown rice-flour shell. It's my take on the quesadilla, only I use brown rice instead of white flour, and nuts and corn instead of meat for the filling. Try one."

The taste of the pie got my stomach juices flowing. I didn't realize how hungry I was. I took a second patty on a napkin while Kurt poured me a very tall mug of coffee.

"We only have soy milk, is that okay?" he said. "Becka did the shopping."

She grinned in a satisfied way. I accepted the milk and went into the living room. The cart was in the middle of the room. It was awesome.

"See," Kurt said. "I built it out of aluminum, to make it light. Gluing and pop riveting the pieces was a bitch, but it was worth it, it looks so cool."

The box, maybe three feet by four and four feet high, gleamed. The rivets were set in even rows and the top was stainless steel with scallops, giving it an art deco look. There was a brightly colored canvas canopy that had jewels and shells sewn into it.

"The grill is cast iron for even heat distribution," he went on. "But check *this* out."

Kurt opened a hatch on a narrow side. He pointed to a steel cylindrical container with copper tubing coming out the top. "It's an old beer keg Josh got me," he said. "Five finger discount."

Kurt explained that he filled the keg with used cooking oil that was filtered and aerated. He used CO_2 to put the oil under pressure, which ran up to the nozzles and squirted out just like a furnace.

"It makes a shit load of kilo-calories," he said. He pointed to one of the copper tubes. "This one feeds a double oven. I have one for warming, one for baking."

The engineering was impressive, and I told Kurt he should get it written up somewhere. He explained that most carts use compressed natural gas because it burns so clean and well. He decided to recycle cooking oil, like he does with his car. "I already have a supply chain for the McDiesel, so Becka can tap into it easy. The hard part was getting the fuel to aerate and control the release pressure to get it to burn completely."

He showed me the other side of the cart, which was refrigerated. "I use the same cooking oil to run the cooling unit, too." This seemed like an impossible feat, but he said campers had used compressed natural gas to run refrigerators in cabins for decades. "It's an old technology," he said. "I just adapted the fuel."

Kurt made it sound like brilliant engineering was as simple as baking a pie, substituting a few ingredients.

"Becka's going to start selling this evening. We'll pull the cart to the Heights and sell them to the tourists walking on the promenade."

Marty came out of the bedroom. He cut a dashing figure in his EMT uniform, all lean and lanky. I could understand why women fell for guys in a uniform. I imagined joining a crack military organization, *The Web Design Battalion*. It wouldn't do any good, women would still see that I was ugly.

"Hey, Pete," Marty said. "Would you hang out with Becka on the Promenade for awhile? I won't get off till after midnight, and Josh has to work. It'll be you and Kurt."

Kurt said he was going to buy some of the quesadillas and walk around exclaiming, "Best pie I ever ate! Best food in the *woild*." He put on a Three Stooges type accent for *world*. I sipped my coffee and complained about being way behind in my work.

Becka said she understood and she was okay without me, but Marty had to work and it would be great if a familiar face stopped by.

It occurred to me that my friends *had* been awfully good to me. So I agreed to go over. "What time should I be there?"

"Five o'clock is the plan," said Kurt.

I was turning to go when Josh came into the room. He had an unlit cigarette hanging from his mouth and sleep in his eyes. He poured a very tall mug of coffee and added a shot of Jack Daniels, muttering, "Coffee, whiskey and weed. An earthly paradise."

I looked at Marty.

"My brother's working on a new play. He's got as far as the title."

Josh opened the fridge and searched for milk.

"Soy? All we've got is fricking *soy* milk?

"It's good for you, bro'," said Marty.

"So is celibacy. Doesn't mean I'm gonna practice it." He poured a tiny amount of soy milk into his coffee. "It isn't even *white*."

"Neither is Carlyle, and it doesn't bother you."

"Carlyle is two years old. I'm talking about the second elixir of life. After god made spirits—I'm talking about the distilled kind—as compensation for mortality, he made coffee. The goat herd in Ethiopia who discovered it added milk from the goats, and the rest is history."

Marty shook his head at his brother's theatrical expressions, while Josh took a long pull on his coffee and lit his cigarette. I told Becka I'd see her on the promenade and went out to the local bodega for bacon, eggs and cheese on a roll. With ketchup.

FIFTEEN

After a second cup of strong coffee—four tablespoons of instant—I tried to work at the computer, but the bed kept pulling me back to sleep. To sleep, perchance to stream. I'd probably dream of Angie rising on an ocean swell, her hair garlanded with sea flowers, her neck hung with seaweed strands, and then a shark from *Jaws* would grab her from below, toss her side to side a few times and pull her under.

My waking nightmares were enough to drive me to the roof and off into space. A running jump, cycle my legs while arcing high into the air, then look down like in the cartoons and realize there was nothing below me, and *whup,* down I go.

Better to try burying my mind in work. I turned on my computer and checked my email. There were a couple million new messages. A guy from Delaware who had a site for collectible diner menus from all over the country wanted to know why his web site hadn't been launched yet. I hadn't finished the links to the gazillion menus, each one was a separate j-peg file. Talk about tedious work.

Two hours of blood and sweat and I had his web site up and running. All the links worked. I emailed the guy to tell him and attached my bill.

I looked at the picture of Angie with the Russian word *rusalka* that I'd scrawled across the glass with a marker. I'd shot the photo through the big front window at Artistry. She was cutting a woman's hair and laughing, the woman must have told her a joke or a funny story. Her head was thrown back and she had so much glee in her face, it always made me smile to see her like that. Now the picture made me want to bang my head against the wall until I passed out. The pain would be so much easier to take than looking at her picture knowing Angie was dead.

Then I had a really chilling thought. Had the police found her body yet? I'd emailed them all that information, they must have found something. I logged on to the Daily News web site and scanned it for news of another female murder victim, but there was no mention of another body. Likewise the Post and the New York Times had nothing. I did a quick run at the Medical Examiner's database, but there were no new Jane Does there, either.

Bad girls *are mermaids.* Svetlana'a words sent chills through me. The bastards had dumped her at sea with the proverbial cement overshoes. I pictured her beautiful body swelling in the inky water, crabs eating her eyes, fish chewing on her flesh. The images were horrifying, but I couldn't stop my mind from making them.

I wish I hadn't promised to help Becka with the McVeggie Kart, now all I wanted was to stay locked inside my room and never talk to another soul again. Maybe throw out the furniture and paint the floor and walls and ceilings an ochre color to make it look like Mars. I could keep the air conditioner set at sixty degrees and make the place feel arctic.

They were good friends, Marty and Becka and Kurt and Josh. It wouldn't be right disappointing them. A promise is a promise.

Becka was smiling that ethereal smile of hers as she loaded stuffed pastries into the McVeggie Kart's little oven. She wore a T-shirt that said *Becka's Bistro – Fresh with Flavor.*

Maybe she wasn't a genius with ad copy, but the smell was great and she looked like a million bucks standing there on the Brooklyn Promenade.

"Hi, Pete!" she called to me. "I've had my first customer! Isn't that wonderful?"

"Success is assured," I told her. "What do you want me to do?"

She asked me to hand out fliers on the promenade. The walkway had lots of people sauntering by and enjoying the view across the East River to lower Manhattan. Boats were tootling along the water. An orange ferry boat out in the greater harbor was leaving a wide wake that got a pair of sailboats bobbing as they crossed the watery furrows.

New Yorkers were out chasing their dreams. It seemed like I was the only one running from a nightmare, but looks can be deceiving. Maybe the young couple with the twins in the double stroller were con artists using their kids in the sting. Could be the business guy in a sharply tailored suit and designer sun glasses was stealing his customers blind.

Becka made a couple more sales. She was smiling and humming a little song, until she saw a female cop coming her way. Suddenly her face sagged. She twisted her apron in her hand as the cop approached. Looking nervous is never a good idea when dealing with the police. I went over to the cart just as the cop reached her.

The lady officer sniffed the air. She was pudgy, with her bullet-proof vest puffing out her chest and leaving her without any bosom to admire.

"What's ya cooking with?" she said.

"Oh, we burn used cooking oil for our grill."

The cop eyed me as I stood with my bundle of flyers.

"Is the homeless guy working for you?" she asked Becka.

"Pete? He's not homeless, he's a friend of mine."

"Man is in serious need of a bath."

Becka said in a low voice, "He's depressed."

"Honey, the whole city is depressed." Then she asked to see the permit.

Becka took the permit out from a cabinet stuffed with food. It was laminated; that had been Kurt's idea. The officer looked at it, turned it over, scanned the back, then she handed it back to Becka.

"You're not supposed to seal it in plastic."

"That was my idea," I said. "I was afraid the grease and the heat would stain the paper."

"Yeah, well when you renew it, just put the thing in a plastic folder. Okay?"

"Sure. Thanks." As the officer turned away, Becka said, "Would you like to try my sweet potato puffs? I use whole wheat flour in the crust."

"Yeah, okay, but just one, I'm watching my weight."

Becka scooped a pastry into a paper napkin and handed it to her. The officer went on her way, one hand holding the food, the other hooked on her belt.

I went back to handing out leaflets. The stack was just about gone when a hand tapped me lightly on the shoulder. I turned around, and there was Jyoti smiling at me with that radiant look on her face.

"Uh, hi," I said. Always the dazzling conversationalist.

"Peter. Becka told me you were helping her first day. That's so sweet."

"Yeah, well..."

While Jyoti and Becka chatted I kicked myself for not combing my hair. Or bathing. Or putting on clean clothes. Or...The list of failures was too long to think about without making me want to jump into the river and drown.

Jyoti turned and began walking along the promenade. The East River glistened in the evening sun. A tugboat tooted like in a children's story. I glanced at Jyoti, who was staring across toward Jersey. Or maybe she was looking farther, toward California, like that old New Yorker cartoon.

"Hard to believe the old wooden boats used to line up two deep all along the waterfront," I told her.

"That was before all the trucks and planes."

"And the cars. They're what killed the harbor."

I wanted to run my fingers through her long black hair. Her dark eyes glistened with the light reflected off the water. I felt as if her eyes could rebuild me into somebody new and pure.

"The weather forecast is a clear sky tonight," she said, looking up at the few lazy clouds.

"Are you flying somewhere?"

She smiled. "You promised to show me the stars. Remember?"

"Yes."

"It will be a clear night."

"Yes, it'll be clear. I didn't forget. I have an appointment for tonight," I said, silently cursing myself for making the 'date' with Svetlana. Jyoti looked disappointed, which stung me hard. "I could break the appointment."

"I wouldn't want you to do that."

"It's no problem," I said, taking out my cell phone. "It's a business meeting. I can make it for another day."

"No, that's okay, I have somebody I have to see anyway. Let me take a rain check."

"Okay." I put away my phone.

She took my hand and squeezed it, saying, "I'll check the weather forecast every day. The next clear night, I'll be over." She released my hand and walked off. I watched her slim figure. She moved like a dancer, smooth and graceful, light on her feet, as if she could leap up on the cement railing and walk along it like a ballerina in a show.

I kept watching until she descended some stairs and disappeared.

SIXTEEN

The sun was teasing the horizon, casting the last pink and orange rays across the sky as I waited for Svetlana to arrive. I was nervous about seeing her without knowing why. Maybe it was like Sartre said; that we're totally free to do anything. Walk out on a bridge and there's nothing keeping you from jumping but your own free will. Hire an escort and there's nothing keeping me from betraying my feelings for Angie but a sense of moral obligation.

Pretty weak stuff to hold back an ocean of desire.

I heard the buzzer at my door sound, looked at the computer monitor. It was Svetlana, right on time. She stuck her tongue out at the camera and waved.

I went to the door to let her in. As soon as I opened the door she rushed up to me, wrapped her arms around me and kissed me on the mouth. Then she laid her head against my chest and said, "It is so good to see you, Petrov. I miss you every day."

I rubbed her back for a minute, feeling her body against mine. She folded her legs around me and nestled. Her perfume tickled my nose. It was sweet, but not too sweet.

She looked up into my eyes. "Do you want go to concert? Or do you want stay in apartment?"

I told her I wanted to go hear the music. She uncoiled her body and and took my hand. "We will go," she said.

Svetlana was dressed in pointed, black, high heeled shoes—the kind that are in fashion this year so all the woman buy them and next year it'll be round and stubby—black stockings, a short skirt, a top that was slinky and taut and cut low enough to invite me to bury my face between her breasts, and a short black leather jacket.

We walked to the club, it was only six blocks from my place. The Brooklyn Poetry Place was a long, narrow storefront with a stage at the back, street art hanging on the walls, and free papers from a dozen art and music groups on a rack by the door. The bar was a formica and chrome affair right out of the fifties; the drinks, heavy on bourbon and Guinness.

There was a performance artist just beginning her set, a young white woman with a bone in her nose like out of some old black and white safari movie, which was totally weird, but it's New York. I guess she was making a statement of some kind.

The woman started some kind of strange dance. The music was this atonal, piercing sound from her MP3 player linked to the sound system. You couldn't tell what kind of instruments had made it. Probably electronically generated.

The woman got down on the floor of the stage and started moaning and keening, not exactly in time with the music, but more or less in sync. Her limbs writhed and her fingers waved like curling limbs of some undersea creature.

"Peter, whut is this mean?" she asked me.

I shrugged. "Symbolism of some kind, I guess."

Svetlana stared at the woman, not knowing what to make of her.

I leaned close to her and said, "Listen,about the other day, I was in the escort service and I asked you about my fr—"

Svetlana had thrust her hand toward my face and placed a finger over my lips. Her eyes grew wide and her brow, furrowed. She leaned in to me, put her lips to my ear and whispered so softly I could barely hear her, "They hear everything," she whispered in a shaky voice.

She removed her finger from my lips and sat back. Her shoulders sagged as she stared at her lap, no longer interested in the performer.

After a moment I made some small talk about the show and the music. She smiled and focused on the performer. The more I made banal conversation the more relaxed she became. Every once in a while she would look around the room, as if there was somebody she knew hanging around.

I thought about writing questions down on paper, but it was a safe bet her English wasn't great, and in the dark she probably wouldn't be able to read them, anyway.

When the show was over, Svetlana asked, "We go to your apartment?"

I looked at her, lovely and young and fragile. I knew that her bosses expected her to end up in bed with me. More services, more charges. But no way was I going to let some creep in a dark room listen to me and Svetlana together, and I didn't like the idea of faking another sex act.

As we went out onto the street I put my finger to my lips, winked, and started walking with my arm around her. Three blocks on we came to the stairs to the subway. I winked again and led her down the steps. We waited for the train.

"Where do we go?"

"Oh, I like to ride the train and watch the tunnel. You can see it coming at you or leaving you behind. If I'm in a good mood I ride in the front; if I'm in a bad mood, I watch the darkness behind me." I looked to see if she was following me. "Does that make sense?"

"It is sense for you, Petrov. That is okay for me."

I liked the way she put a Russian spin on my name. She let the 'v' vibrate a little, like a singer holding a note at the end of a phrase. It was sexy.

As we heard the rumble of the train and felt a breeze rise up ahead of the oncoming train, I asked did she want to ride in the first car or the last. She had no opinion, so I took the last, anticipating bad news.

In the last car there was only an old guy asleep leaning into the corner. We sat by the back window and watched the station disappear around a curve. It was like an amusement park ride. We twisted with the curves and jerked forward and back. The hills were nothing to brag about, but it was still a terrific ride.

Over the rattle of the train I explained, “The transmitter you’re wearing won’t function in the subway.”

Svetlana’s mouth fell open, hearing me speak openly of the device she had divulged to me.

“You are sure, Petrov? You know this is true?”

“Yeah. I’m pretty good with computer stuff.” I leaned in close to her and softly said, “Whisper in my ear if you’re not sure.”

I asked her about Pearl: was she the big boss? Did she decide what happened to the girls? At first Svetlana was afraid to talk. At each stop she looked to see who got on the train.

Finally she said, “Pearl is bad woman. Vury bad. Evil woman.”

“What’s so bad about her?”

“You see her snake?”

I told her I had seen one in a tank in the waiting room.

“That was baby. Where do you think is mother?”

A hideous image came to my mind of Pearl threatening Angie with a snake.

“She has, how you say, shock stick?“

“A cattle prod?”

“Dah. Like for cattle. She uses on snake to get it off girl. If Pearl think she cheat with money, girl is locked in room with snake. Snake wrap around girl’s chest and throat and...”

“Damn.” An image of Angie being smothered by a boa constrictor sent shivers through me. It was sadistic. Evil, like a prison guard with no restrictions. Guantanamo stuff.

"What about Angie? Did they threaten her with the snakes?"

She shrugged her slender shoulders. "I do not know. Maybe. Angie is gone. I think she is in the sea. That is where all girls go when they are no good for work any more."

"They told you this? They said they bury the women in the ocean?"

Tears welling up in her eyes, she nodded, too choked up to speak. She buried her face in my chest and wept. I stroked her hair and tried to comfort her.

When she stopped crying, I said softly, "Come home and stay with me. Quit the place."

"I can not. They have my sister and my mother back in Odessa. They will do bad things if I run away."

"Maybe they can come to the States."

"You have so much money? And I have no papers, they take my passport. I have nothing. I will be sent back home and I will be killed dead."

She leaned her face against my chest. I reached down and stroked her hair, feeling a wave of tenderness. When I touched her cheek, I discovered it was wet.

"It's okay, Svetlana. I'll take care of you."

She kissed my hand, looked up at me. Her eyes were glistening with a fatalism, like someone going to the gallows but with head held high.

We rode the subway to the end of the line and back again to my neighborhood. As we got up to exit the car, I asked her one last time to come home with me, but she shook her head in sadness, not even saying the words.

The climb to the street felt like we were going to a funeral. Outside my building a black Lincoln Town Car was waiting for her. She saw it, stopped walking, and stood frozen in place.

I kissed her passionately good-bye, and I wasn't faking it. I felt a rush of compassion and love for her. It was a powerful emotion running through me. I wanted to scoop her up and carry her into the building. But all I could do was kiss her and tell her everything would be all right.

When she approached the car, the passenger door opened. She saw a figure inside, gasped, and slowly eased her body into the car. I couldn't make out who was in the seat waiting for her, the windows were darkened. I watched the car pull away, kicking myself for letting her go, feeling powerless and a total failure. Again.

SEVENTEEN

I was checking my email, thinking about Svetlana riding away in the car and kicking myself for letting her go. I imagined myself going back to the escort service and demanding to see Svetlana again. Like there was any chance they would give her to me.

I wasn't focusing on the email, my mind wandering, when movement on the video display caught my eye. A bulky figure was coming down the hallway toward my door. As I stared at the screen watching the big guy coming straight at my door, I suddenly realized he was the same guy who left Angie's apartment the night her computer went dead. And as he stood outside my door looking up and down the hall, like he was checking to be sure nobody was watching, his hand went inside his jacket and to his waistline. I didn't need anyone to tell me he was reaching for a gun, he had the flat face and dead eyes of a guy who took no joy in his work, but killed coldly because it was a job.

I ran to the bedroom, closed the door and locked it, and rushed to the window. Just as I threw a leg over onto the fire escape I heard a loud *crash*: the mob guy had broken the door down and was coming my way.

As I squeezed my body through the bedroom window and stepped onto the fire escape, I looked down and saw the six flights to the ground—too far away for me to reach it before mister thug got to the window and started squeezing off shots. The penthouse was only one flight up—a no-brainer. I scrambled up the metal stairs to the parapet and heaved my body over. I stood up, leaned over and looked down. Thug guy was sticking his head out of my window. He had a thick neck and was pointing a gun at me. I couldn't help thinking, *what a walking cliché.* I pulled back and ran for the door to Marty's apartment a few yards away. I turned the knob. It was open! Good old Marty; he trusted his neighbors.

I locked the door behind me and called out, "*Anybody home?*" Kurt answered from his room.

"Kurt! I've got a problem! There's a guy after me. With a gun!"

Kurt put down the charcoal pencil he was using to draw at his easel and raced to his room, calling, "*Who is he?*"

"I don't know, but he looks awful unfriendly."

"Knock on Marty's door, he's sleeping in from a long shift!"

I knocked and opened the door. Marty was curled up like a ball, with Becka's arms wrapped around him from behind. I didn't have time to admire their sweet embrace. "Marty! I have a problem!"

Marty opened his eyes and sat bolt upright. He looked around the room, then focused his eyes on me.

"Pete, what's up? Are you sick?"

"No, there's a thug broke into my apartment. I'm afraid he might follow me up here. He has a gun."

Realizing that I had put my friends in danger, I started to apologize for bringing the problem into his lap, but he waved me off. Becka was awake now. She and Marty got out of bed. They were both naked, and they pulled on clothes as if they didn't care that I was in the room; as if nudity was a natural state for them.

In the living room Kurt was standing with an arrow pulled taut against the string of a weird-looking bow. He indicated his foil standing beside him with his eyes. Marty picked it up and stepped to the door to the roof.

"Nobody outside," Marty said.

I looked at the bow and arrow in Kurt's hands, puzzled.

"It's a Mongolian weapon. They're just as powerful as the English long bow, even though they're half the weight and size."

Becka went to the front door and opened the peephole.

"Don't stand in front of the door," Marty told her.

"Nobody outside," she said, stepping to the side.

Becka opened her cell phone. "I'm dialing 911," she said.

"Wait a sec, we should discuss this," said Marty.

"What's there to discuss? Our lives are in danger. We need the police to arrest the man with the gun."

"I don't know," said Kurt. "If you call the cops they'll want to know about Pete's thing with Angie. He has these photos on his computer from the Medical Examiner that are kind of illegal."

Becka looked at me, phone in hand. "He has a *gun*."

"True. But we have weapons, too. I just—"

Becka looked through the peephole again. "There's a guy coming up the hall!" she said.

"What does he look like?" I asked.

"He's bald, he's wearing a sports coat and slacks, shirt and tie. The tie is ugly."

"Is he a big guy with a barrel chest?"

"No, he's not that big," said Becka. "He looks more like a—"

"*POLICE! OPEN UP!*"

". . . cop," she finished.

"Shit, I know that voice. That's Detective Gisondi." I approached the door. As Becka reached for the lock, I said, "How did he find out where I am?"

Detective Gisondi stood in the middle of the living room, shaved head and a gold earring in his ear. He wasn't a big guy, but he had a swagger and he projected a sense of power that was intimidating. I had the feeling he didn't have to rely on his gun to make himself understood.

Assigning two uniformed cops to the hallway and roof, Gisondi looked at Kurt, who had unsprung his bow and arrow, and Marty, who planted the tip of the foil on the floor.

"Looks like you guys are ready to rumble," said Gisondi. "What's the problem?"

I could see the yearning to speak in Becka's eyes. I glanced at Marty, who shrugged, noncommittal. Kurt kept a poker face.

"I had an unwanted visitor in my apartment," I told him. "He was scary. I came up here for help."

"I figured that was why you scrambled up the fire escape. You were moving pretty fast."

"Didn't you see the guy with the gun?" I asked.

"What guy was that?"

That set off alarms in my head. The mob guy had poked his head out the window with a gun in his hand. If the cops couldn't see something that big and ugly, what good were they?

"Let's go down to your apartment and sort this out," said Gisondi. He instructed the uniformed cops to take statements from my friends, then he led me down to my apartment. The front door was open, the door frame splintered where it had been broken open. He stepped past the broken lock without a comment.

Inside, he stood in the middle of the living room and looked around. Right away he saw several pictures of Angie. They showed her in her apartment across the street, at work, and in a restaurant. There was one with her trying on a pair of shoes at a little shop in the West Village. I loved seeing her with bare feet.

"Your girlfriend?" he asked.

"Not exactly."

"What was she to you? *Exactly*."

I felt my throat tighten. Here it was. Cops were good at sensing a lie.

"Angie was a neighbor."

"You took that picture from your window," he said, looking across the street.

"Yes."

This got his attention. He looked me up and down as if I were a specimen in a jar. He looked around the room and saw the telescope.

"Did you use that?" he asked.

"No. I have a telephoto lens on my camera. I use the telescope to look at the stars."

He nodded his head as if the two types of photography made sense to him.

"Look. You're the guy who sent me the email photos of the dead girl. Right?"

I didn't answer him.

"I recognize your voice."

When I still kept mum, he warned me they had my conversation on tape and they could do a voice analysis to prove it was me. I had a hunch he was lying. I didn't think they recorded *every* phone call they received, but since 9/11 New York has received a lot of money for surveillance technology, so maybe it was true.

"You called me and said your friend was dead. That she was dumped down near the ocean in Brooklyn. Right?"

I admitted I'd made the call. "Did you find out who she is?" I asked.

Gisondi let a smirk play on his face. "I ask the questions, you answer them." He saw a photo album on a book shelf and reached for it.

"Don't you need a warrant or something?"

"Plain sight," he said, opening the album. It was filled with pictures of Angie. Some were at her job at Artistry, others were of her at restaurants, an art show, walking in the park.

"You really had a hard-on for her." Looking up from the photos, he said, "You were stalking her."

I started to sweat. The sweat dripped from my arm pits onto my flanks and ran down. I really wanted to help the detective, he had the resources to find Angie's killer. At the same time, I never trusted cops. They had beat me up too many times when I was living with my mom, and they beat on her, too. A rock and a hard place...

"No, it was nothing like that. One morning when I finished my work I looked out on the street, just to see what was going on in the neighborhood, and I saw her leaning out her apartment window and looking up at the sky, like she was checking the weather. And then she looked down at the street. I found that interesting. I sort of made her morning routine part of mine. After seeing her go off to work I would wrap up my projects and go to bed."

"But you *followed* her. It's all right here in the pictures."

"Look, I'm a photojournalist. All my pictures are taken in public, just like anyone else in the business."

"You ever post your photos on the web?"

"No."

"Submit them for publication in a magazine?"

I shook my head. It felt like my head weighed a hundred pounds and if I shook it too far it would keep on spinning around until it snapped my neck.

"I was going to submit some of my stuff. I wasn't ready, yet, that's all."

Gisondi studied my face as I spoke. He was running an internal program that assessed my truthfulness. There are algorithms that count how many times you stammer or repeat yourself or blink. They can even measure the size of your pupil. When it dilates, you're lying.

"I saw her carrying a bag with the logo from her job, so I went to the hairdressers a couple of times."

"And when she didn't poke her head out the window, that's when you got worried."

"I figured she was away on vacation or staying with a friend."

"You ever see a male in her apartment?"

"No. Once in a while a girlfriend stayed the night. That didn't happen too often."

"Think she was gay?"

"It occurred to me."

"How'd you feel about that?"

Trying not to hesitate and indicate I was fabricating a story, I told him honestly, "The thought turned me on."

GIsondi smirked. "So lemme get this straight. You were watching this girl for a while, and you notice she doesn't show in the window for, what, a couple of days?"

"Five."

"Five days. So you call me up and want to report her missing, but you don't really *know* she's missing."

A uniformed cop was looking at my computer. When I told him not to mess with it, Gisondi told me he had a court order to seize it. Although I was relieved we'd used Kurt's computer to hack into the Medical Examiner's database, I did have copies of Tasha'a photo from the autopsy. That was going to be tough to explain. Maybe my firewalls and poison pill program would protect me when they hacked into my computer. Probably not.

"The neighborhood is a village, we all eat at the same places most of the time," I said.

Gisondi scowled in disgust. It was obvious he wasn't buying my story.

"You know what I think? I think you were stalking these women. I think you're a lowlife pervert who stalks women.

I think you killed them and you sent their photos to dare us to catch you." As I opened my mouth to protest, Gisondi added, "You're coming down to the precinct with me, and you're not coming back for forty years. If ever."

EIGHTEEN

I was in an interrogation room, not a holding cell, trying to find comfort in not being handcuffed. It was a gray room with a metal table and chairs and a sense of despair, like a lot of rooms I'd spent time in. Juvie hall. Security office in the high school for the social rejects.

Sitting alone in that gray room for what felt like days gave me time to think about Angie and about her being dead and my not being able to protect her. And the more I thought about my failures and how empty my life was without her, the more spending time in jail didn't seem all that bad. They could execute me and bury me in a shallow grave; they could throw me in solitary for the rest of my life with bread and water without even a bird to visit my window—what did it matter? Without Angie I was less than nothing.

There was a mirror on the wall beside the door. It had to be a one-way mirror. Gisondi could be out there right now sipping a cup of coffee and watching me. Wasn't that my life? Watching people from a vantage point that kept me invisible? That was why Angie had died. She didn't know me so she couldn't reach out and ask for my help, and I never gave her a chance to share her story with me.

Mom had been right. I was a *sneaky Pete.* Only now there was nobody to call me out from behind the stuffed chair and give me a quarter to go outside and play in the park. Now I was on my own and in deep, dark shit.

I looked at my hands. They looked weird, like they were deformed. When I bent the fingers into a fist, it felt like they belonged to somebody else's hand. I watched them to see if the fists would start pounding my face. Beat some sense into me. It would be a relief to feel them cracking my nose, the pain in my heart wouldn't be so great.

After waiting for what felt like hours, I was brought up short by the door opening without a knock. In walked Detective Gisondi. He was carrying my photo album, a box of framed photos from my apartment, and my telescope. When he leaned the telescope in the corner without spreading the tripod legs, I worried it would fall over and crack the lens.

The detective watched me for several minutes without speaking. Probably checking my body language. That was funny, since my body was acting like it had a different owner. My hands definitely belonged to somebody else, and my head had this echo inside it, like there was a wind blowing through it. Or somebody's breath.

Thumbing through the photos, Gisondi said, "The DA tells me he's got an open and shut case of stalking."

He said it like he was casually mentioning the weather report. He watched me for a moment. I looked at my hands hoping they would go back to being mine again.

"Am I boring you?" he said.

"No, sorry. I'm not feeling well."

"I asked you why you took pictures of Angie and Tasha, and you were telling me some bullshit about being a photojournalist. You're gonna have to do a lot better than that if you don't want to spend twenty-five to life upstate."

He held my photo album open toward me and turned the pages. They were filled with photos of Angie, sometimes with Tasha or other women. Studying the photos, a sudden breath of hope blew over me: Gisondi hadn't brought in any photos from my hard drive, where I had way more pictures of

Angie, plus the images of Tasha's body Kurt got for me from the Medical Examiner's computer. The police hadn't gotten into my computer; my *poison pill program had worked!*

"This you call *art*?" he said.

I said, "That's right. I make compositional art. What's wrong with that?"

"They're all women."

"No they're not. There are men in a lot of my pictures."

"Oh, sure, a couple of passersby. But the focus is always on a female."

"There's a cute dog in that one." I stabbed a photo of a sidewalk scene.

"It's a young woman walking a dog," he said.

"There's a lovely view of Manhattan in the background," I added, making no impression.

He got up and went to the telescope, spread the legs and turned the lens toward me. He even pretended to look in the lens, but I was way too close for him to focus my image in the eyepiece.

"I gotta tell you, Pete, this is some serious shit," he said, still pretending to look into the lens.

"What do you mean?"

"This thing is perfect for peeping into bedrooms."

"That's bull. You saw my photos. I never took a picture of a naked woman. Not once."

"So you say."

"You didn't find any, did you?"

"We only started looking at your computer. We'll find them."

The fact that he was still hoping to find scurrilous pictures on my hard drive convinced me my protection software had worked. My files were safe for now, which would buy me a little time.

"You can look at my computer all you want, you won't

find any dirty pictures. All of my shots are of people in their clothes in public. If I want nude shots I can download hundreds of them from the web."

Gisondi scratched his chin. "You got another prob' here, my friend. A big one."

"Oh?"

"You're facing a Homeland Security rap." He tapped the telescope.

"That's ridiculous. I'm not a terrorist."

"In this climate all it takes is a telescope and a view of Manhattan, which you have, and the Feds sit up and take notice. You could be studying airplane landing patterns. Truck routes. Federal buildings. All kinds of shit."

Gisondi leaned forward and stared into my eyes. "You could end up in Guantanamo, no name, no number. Just a body dropped in a hole where nobody can hear you scream."

Up until now the prospect of years in jail hadn't bothered me too much, crazy as it sounds, I'd been in juvie detention more than once. But the thought of being swallowed up in the American gulag sent a wave of fear through me. No communication with the outside world. *No internet access.* If Gisondi was trying to scare me into talking, he was doing a damn good job of it.

"There is nothing in my computer or in my apartment that has the slightest hint of terrorist activity."

"Not any more there isn't." He pulled his chair closer and leaned forward. An illusion of intimacy. "You know something? I believe you about the Homeland stuff. But the Feds have itchy trigger fingers.They presume you're guilty and you have to prove you're innocent. That's tough to do when you're in permanent solitary."

I made my eyes like slits and leaned into him. Two could play the tough guy.

"You're leaving out one important fact."

"What's that?"

"If you give me to the Feds, you won't get any more information out of me about Tasha and Angie."

Gisondi smiled a Mona Lisa smile that made me believe the critics who claimed Da Vinci painted himself in drag. "Just what makes you think we really care all that much about a couple of dead hookers?"

Gisondi left me alone again to stew on his threat about turning me over to the Feds. If he thought his cavalier attitude toward her death and Tasha's would rattle me, he was right. They had to investigate the murders of two women, but how far they pushed it was fluid.

They never filed criminal charges against anyone in my aunt's death. Another hooker beaten to death in her own bed. Who cared? My mom was too sick with AIDS to protest, and I was too young to do anything about it except act out and get put away myself.

The more I tried to figure out what to do, the more everything got into a mush. My head throbbed, my ass was sore, and my hands were numb. I lay my head down on my arms and closed my eyes. The room started to spin; I felt like I was going to fall out of my chair and get flushed down a drain.

Maybe I would slip into a coma and never have to speak to Gisondi or anybody else again. I wondered if there was some way I could induce a coma without banging my head so hard it really killed me.

My mind followed this crazy idea for some time, until my eyes grew too heavy to keep open. Without tooth picks to prop them open, I let them fall shut.

NINETEEN

Without a clock on the wall or my cell phone, which the cops had taken, there was no telling how long I was half asleep. The door unlocking and opening roused me. A uniformed guard held the door open. An old guy who looked like Walter Matthau sober came in. He wore a rumpled suit and carried a battered leather brief case that looked like it had seen as many years as he had. The guy held out his hand to me. It was leathery and strong.

"Ira Goldstein," he said. "I'll be representing you."

"But how..."

"I'll explain everything once we're out of here. I've already spoken with the District Attorney. I pointed out that he has absolutely no evidence whatsoever that you were connected to the murder of that poor unfortunate woman who was found out by Floyd Bennett field, or to the disappearance of her friend, Angela Andrews."

"The mob guy was going to kill me!"

"I made that point abundantly clear to him. You'll be going before the judge in a few minutes. Just tell her 'Not guilty' when she asks what is your plea. I think I can get you out on a reasonable amount of bail."

"I don't have a lot of money, Mister Goldstein. A few hundred bucks in the bank, and —"

"Relax, your bail is covered."

I didn't understand what he meant by "covered," but he was warm and confident and I felt I could trust him.

"Detective Gisondi threatened to turn me over to the Homeland Defense people. He said I could be using my telescope to track flight patterns."

"He was just trying to scare you, the DA hates the Feds. He wants this case for himself."

"But what am I being charged with?"

"Stalking, invasion of privacy, talking too loud in the public library, it's all bullshit charges. They're blowing a lot of smoke on the murder of that hooker."

"Tasha."

""That's the one."

"I gave them her name and where she worked!"

"Is that right?" Goldstein chuckled. I noticed he made no notes as we talked. He was either such an old pro that he kept all the facts sorted out in his mind, or he made it up as he went along.

"We don't have to worry about the murder charges. I'll settle the stalking issue and have you out of here."

A uniformed officer opened the door and gestured for us to follow him.

"Time to meet the judge," said Goldstein. We followed the uniformed cop to learn my fate.

As I walked with my lawyer through a maze of corridors, I said in a whisper, "I don't have a lot of money at the moment. I might be able to sell some computer equipment or something "

"Relax. Your friends put up the money. Just plead not guilty and let me do the talking."

The cop led us to a large room with a secretary, a desk with a bored looking officer seated up high, an old white woman in judge's robes seated behind a desk. The judge kept writing in a book without looking up or acknowledging me.

When my case was called up, the judge asked me how did I plead. The charge was criminal stalking in the fourth degree. The District Attorney claimed I was a pervert who took clandestine photos of the deceased. He laid out a dozen photos for the judge to look over.

"I don't see anything prurient here," the judge said. "These look more like tourist shots."

"Mr. Davies has a telescope we believe he used to observe one of the women in the photos."

"You have the pictures?"

"Not at this time, your honor. Our I-T people are still working with the accused's computer."

Mr. Goldstein gave me a questioning look. I whispered in his ear that I had a very robust security program. When the police technician tried to get past my password protocol, a Trojan horse would wipe the entire drive clear in less than a minute: a complete meltdown.

The judge handed the photos back. "No prurient photos. I assume you have a complaining witness."

"Uh, no, your honor. One of the women in the photo, a Tasha Gordon, was brutally murdered. We have reason to believe that a second victim, Miss Angelina Andrews, may also have been killed."

"Because *my* client provided you with that information," Goldstein said. "Your honor, Mister Davies sent the police department photos of the two women and a letter explaining his concern. He himself was nearly killed by the member of a criminal gang who broke into his apartment and threatened him with a gun."

"And he gave all this evidence to the police during his interrogation?"

"Yes, your honor."

The two lawyers batted the ball across the net a few more times. When the judge asked if the DA was prepared to charge me with murder, he was told that the District Attorney's office was actively pursuing that possibility, but was not ready to bring the case before a grand jury. That lost him some points. Finally the judge let me go with a bail of fifty thousand dollars.

At the announcement of the bail, I looked at the lawyer with anxiety, but he assured me I only had to put up ten percent, and my friends had already collected that much.

On the way out of the police station we passed several cops coming in. One of them had a familiar swaggering gait: it was one of the two going into the brothel the day I met Svetlana. The cop beside him was his stubby partner.

It looked like the police were investigating the brothel after all. If Gisondi had the escort service under surveillance, he had to know I wasn't involved with any murder. So why charge me and give me so much abuse?

When I finally got out on the street, Mister Goldstein gave me his card and told me to call him in the morning. I looked around, and there were Marty, Kurt and Becka waiting beside Kurt's McDiesel. We hugged and laughed and cursed the cops as we got in and Kurt pulled out in a cloud of fragrant smoke.

On the ride back home, Marty explained that right after the cops took me away, Jyoti happened to call. When Becka told her what happened to me, Jyoti called Mr. Goldstein, who took the case right away. Kurt, Marty and Becka put up the bail money.

"Where is Jyoti? Is she waiting back at the apartment?"

"No," Becka said. "She had to work, but she said she'd call when she was free."

In the interrogation room I'd sunk into a deep pit of despair, not much caring if I lived or died. The generosity of my friends made me kick myself for being so wrapped up in my own shit. They were so positive; so sure that life was worth living and that I was worth helping. Even the smell of the burning vegetable oil in the car's diesel engine and its rough clatter added to their charm and their joy in living.

Becka was trying to make the world a better place with her

food; Kurt was designing things for kids that made them smarter and safer; Marty was keeping them alive on the way to the hospital; and Josh was making beautiful music that touched their souls. What was I doing? Wrapping myself in self-pity and withdrawing from the world. Watching people and never engaging with them. I was pathetic.

My friends were so full of passion for life. So was Jyoti, it showed in everything she said. It was reflected in her smile and in her voice. I had to learn how to latch onto that kind of energy and ride it to a better place.

If only Jyoti was here to teach me.

TWENTY

Back at our building, Kurt took me to my apartment and showed how he and Marty and Josh had fixed my door. The lock was repaired and the inside of the door was lined in stainless steel.

"Dude," Kurt said. "While you were gone I got a sheet of steel from the super—he has so much *great shit* down in the basement, you wouldn't *believe.* Marty and I screwed it into the door. Then I put in one of those old-fashioned twist beam locks. A SWAT team couldn't get past that baby."

We went up to the penthouse, where Becka had put out plates of food. Josh served Guiness. It was fantastic. Marty put some music on and turned the sound off the big television set. Sometimes it almost seemed like the soccer players were in sync with the music.

"You sure pissed somebody off," said Marty. "I know. When I'm on a case and the cops are on your side, they can make things really smooth. But if they think we're getting in their way or poaching on their territory, they can ream you a new asshole and laugh as you shit blood."

"I don't even know what I did. Okay, I visited that escort service, but it's not like I did anything suspicious."

"You're playing with fire, dude," Kurt said. "Keep out of dark alleys, you know what I'm saying?"

Josh said, "If you need a piece for protection, I can get you one."

Marty poked his brother in the arm. "Since when have you joined the NRA?"

"No, there's a guy comes to my club, he deals in everything.

I mean, *everything.* Hot cars, fake diamonds. . .weapons."

I thanked Josh and told him I didn't want to mess around with a gun, I'd probably end up shooting myself in the foot. I preferred to stay out of sight. That was my plan from here on in. Do my work from the computer and keep the door bolted.

When I went back to my apartment I debated staying up the rest of the night or getting some sleep. I was dead tired but wired at the same time. I was looking at my bed through the open door, debating my options, when the buzzer at the door startled me. Okay, mobsters don't buzz, but still...

A glance at the monitor caught me by surprise: *it was Jyoti.* It was really her, standing outside my door.

"Hi, Peter," she said when I got the new lock unbolted and released. "It sounds like you're really locked in good." She noted the steel plate and the bar locking the door as she entered.

"I was just looking through a catalogue at some body armor. It's used stuff, but still pretty much intact."

After thanking her for finding me the lawyer, I pointed out it was a clear night. For New York. "There's actually a lot less soot in the air since the city cracked down on the old oil furnaces that burned the dirtiest fuel on the market."

We went up to the roof with the telescope the cops had returned to me. People talk about the great view of Manhattan from the roof of our building, and it's true, at night the city sparkles like a million stars that fell to earth. But the view of the sky is even better when the wind is off the ocean blowing the smog away.

I pointed the scope at the evening star, not far from a crescent moon, and invited Jyoti to look.

"That's Venus," she said, squinting one eye. "The goddess of love." She had a soft, sexy voice.

I pointed out Virgo just above Venus. She pressed her body close to mine and looked along the line of sight I made with my pointing finger.

When she noted that the planets didn't twinkle the way the stars did, I explained that stars twinkle as the point of light is distorted passing through the atmosphere. A planet projects a disc of light, so its rays are actually made of many points, which results in less distortion.

"It's such a beautiful pure light," she said. "Beautiful."

She looked up at me. "What is it about looking at the stars that you like?"

I felt a powerful urge to let the story run out of me in a big rush of words. To tell her about my loneliness and my solitary nights on the roof, but it wouldn't work. She'd see I was a misfit and a recluse and she'd head for the stairs before I could get half the story out.

"The stars? I don't know. Partly I guess it's because astronomy is such an ancient practice. It goes back thousands of years."

"You feel you're a part of a very old society."

"That's some of it."

"What's the rest of it?"

"Ah, it sounds stupid. You wouldn't understand."

"How do you know that?" Her voice got a little brittle. That surprised me. "How do you know I won't understand you when you know so little about me? Maybe I'm telepathic. Maybe I can read your thoughts and feel your emotions."

"That's science fiction."

"The mind reading part, sure, but some people are very empathic. They feel what others feel."

"That sounds dangerous."

Jyoti smiled that radiant smile of hers. "There's more

danger in closing yourself off from people, Peter. It feels safer, but it's very much worse."

Nobody called me Peter since my mother died. She called me that when she was very angry or very happy with me. I hoped that Jyoti would never be angry with me for anything.

She poked my chest with her finger. "Come on, tell me. What else do you like about gazing at the stars?"

"Honestly? I like to imagine that I'm an astronaut and I'm walking on the surface of Mars. You can't walk on Jupiter, the gravity would kill you instantly."

"That's a wonderful dream. Are you part of some international mission to populate the planet?"

"No, I'm by myself."

Jyoti's smile sank. She got this other look: not anger or disgust, but sadness.

"Peter, you're too good a human being to hide yourself away from everyone."

I didn't say anything about that, there was no point contradicting so obvious a falsehood.

"I mean it," she said. "Look how hard you worked to find your friend. There are very few people in the world who would go that far and risk that much for somebody they loved."

I shrugged. It didn't seem heroic to me, it was just something I had to do. It wasn't something you talked about.

"I'm getting cold," she said. As she stood before me on the dark roof, the crescent moon and the glow from the city lights cast her face in pale light. She was breathlessly beautiful, her long hair a river of darkness, her eyes shining like binary stars.

"I'll make us some hot tea," I said.

We went to my apartment, which for a change was half-way cleaned up. We stood a moment in the middle of the living room. I wanted to grab her and kiss her and drag her to my bed, but I was frozen in place. My feet felt like they were nailed to the floor, with this beautiful woman out of my reach and out of my league.

TWENTY-ONE

As I put the kettle on, Jyoti stepped toward my computer. "We put that software in place that you got for me. It's working really good. Want to see?"

"Uh, Okay."

She typed in the URL. I looked at her hands and saw the knuckles were red and swollen.

"How did you hurt your hand?" I asked.

"Occupational hazard," she said.

We looked over the GirlTalk homepage. Jyoti logged in, and right away we got instant messages appearing in a boxed area labeled ChatterBox. That was a little cute for my taste, but if it worked for them...

There were seventy messages in the queue waiting to be read.

"You've got a busy chat room," I said.

"You can see why one person couldn't edit all of them in a day."

The messages had subject lines like, *Fashionistas hate fat girls,* and *I Got My Groove Back with the Old man.* Another read *Cialis in Paris. Viva la France!* There was a discussion about keeping desire burning in a long term relation versus going outside the relationship for sex. It was racy and honest and real.

From the Home Page she clicked on the Photo Gallery of *Women Taking Charge*. It showed women in all kinds of activities, like spelunking and fossil hunting, flying a small plane and designing clothing. There were a lot of teachers on summer getaways doing cool things.

One picture showed a woman with a streak of gray leading a summer retreat for women. The woman looked familiar. She had been in Hydra with the younger women hanging on her.

““Didn’t I see her at Hydra the other night?”

“Could be. Lot’s of interesting women go there.” She took the mouse and moved to another page. “Peter, Becka told me about the friend you’re worried about.”

I shrugged. It seemed weird talking to her about Angie. I mean, it felt like a betrayal.

“Did your friend say anything about being in trouble? Or where she might go?”

I chewed on my lip, not knowing what to say to her. If I admitted that Angie and I had never spoken, Jyoti would realize I was a creep and head for the door.

“Well,” Jyoti said, “what do you think happened to her? You must have *some* idea.”

I shrugged again. “I don’t know. It’s hard to explain. I don’t really know her that well, she’s more of a neighbor than a close personal friend. I’ve seen her around the neighborhood.”

“I think it’s sweet that you’re worried about her.”

Jyoti looked at me, expecting more. I wanted to satisfy her, but I didn’t want to make her hate me.

“I have a hunch that she was sick, she was going to a hospital clinic.” I didn’t add that it was an STD clinic.

Jyoti continued to look at me and I refused to meet her eyes. Her eyes were dangerous. They were lasers that bore into my mind.

I got up and went to put the tea bags in the pot. I imagined sticking my hand in the hot water and yelling from the pain. It would have distracted me. Stupid idea.

“I don’t like to pry, Peter,” she said as I set down the tea. “I was just wondering why you are so worried about her if you didn’t know her well.”

I shrugged. "Maybe I was waiting for the right moment to talk to her."

I poured the tea and set out sugar and milk. We drank in silence. My hands around the cup felt the heat, and at the same time they seemed to send the sensation somewhere else, like I was feeling a mirror image of a sensation. Weird.

Jyoti closed the site and logged off. She leaned toward me, put her arms around my neck, and kissed me tenderly on the lips. The touch of her mouth was as light as a feather.

She nestled her head on my chest and dropped her arms to my waist. I felt her slim body pressing against me. She was the most sensual woman I'd ever held in my arms.

"Want me to stay?" she asked.

"Uh, I'd like that, sure."

My heart was leaping out of my chest, I wanted her to stay with me so badly. I wanted to hold her in my arms and never let go. We would work out of the apartment and not leave it for weeks. Months. Years. Just the two of us wrapped in each other's arms day and night.

But I knew deep down and without a flicker of doubt that if she got closer to me Jyoti would see the ugly, debased, relic of a man that I really am, and she would run from me in disgust.

I told her I was flat worn out and needed to sleep for twenty-four hours, could she understand that? She said that was okay, she'd tuck me in and stay with me until I fell asleep.

She took my hand and led me to the bedroom, my heart threatening to leap out of my chest. The bed was a mess. She looked at it and shook her head.

"Have you a set of fresh sheets? It would feel so refreshing."

I got out a fresh set from the closet and together we made the bed. That was sexy. I was excited and happy and scared all at the same time.

Spying a candle on a bedside table, Jyoti asked for a match

and lit the candle. I turned out the light and sat on the edge of the bed.

She let her shoes drop off, then she bent down and untied my sneakers. Her long black hair fell across her face as she bent down, and when she pulled my shoes off my feet I was horrified thinking she would smell them and be revolted. Thank god I'd showered that day and put on fresh cotton socks.

Jyoti stood and kissed me again. I held her close to me and we fell onto the bed. We kissed and kissed some more, her mouth and mine in a succulent duet.

With a mischievous smile she unbuttoned my shirt and kissed my chest, saying, "I'm glad you're not all hairy." I'd often wished I had more hair. And more muscle. And washboard abs. But if she liked my spare chest, it was okay with me.

As Jyoti reached down to undo my belt, I felt my desire ebbing. An icy sensation ran through me. The most beautiful girl I'd ever had in my bed ever, and I was losing my steam. In my chest my heart was swelling with love, but below the waist I was fading out.

I reached for her hand and drew it away from my belt. She looked at me, puzzled.

"Too fast?" she said.

"Yes. Let me hold you awhile."

She snuggled into the crook of my arm while I stroked her hair and kissed her face. I was burning to take her and have my way with her, but the brakes were locked and my engine was stalled.

I drew away from her a little and looked into her eyes. She had such warm and tender eyes. They were eyes that could heal a cripple. Why couldn't I let her look at my naked body with joy?

"Jyoti," I said.

"Mmm?" She watched me, waiting to find out what was going on.

"I want you to do something for me. Okay?"

"Anything for you, Peter."

Her words were encouraging. Could I really be holding the girl of my dreams?

"I want you to go out into the living room. Close the bedroom door when you go, and count to ten slowly, like this: one-thousand one, one-thousand, two, one-thousand three. When you get to ten, come into the room, slowly undress yourself, slip under the sheets. Okay?"

Her face showed bewilderment, but gradually her puzzlement turned to comprehension. With a conspiratorial smile, she kissed my nose and went out of the room, closing the door silently behind her.

I went to the closet, stepped in and closed the door, leaving a crack for me to watch through. A moment later Jyoti came back. She stood in the middle of the room, lifted a foot and slowly peeled off a sock. She peeled off the other one, then climbed onto the bed and sat in the middle. With infinite patience she released the buttons of her shirt.

She let the shirt drop from her shoulders. It seemed to flow along her body as it descended to the bed. She reached her hand to her shoulder and pulled the strap down so slowly it was almost cruel. The second strap down, she held the bra in place with one hand and released the clasp behind with the other. Looking down at her chest, she let the bra slip away.

I pulled off my shirt in concert with her, letting it fall to the closet floor in unison with her movements. It was as if we were connected by invisible strings of desire.

Lying back, she released her slacks and peeled them away. I did the same with mine. She was wearing a thong. The sight of it made me crazy. She rolled onto her stomach, showing the most heavenly buttocks in the known world. She slowly lowered the thong to her knees and kicked them off with her foot as I let my briefs drop to the floor.

As naked as the hour of her birth, Jyoti slowly rolled onto her back, pulled the sheet up to her shoulders, closed her eyes and smiled a beguiling smile.

By now crazy with desire, I went to her, eased myself beneath the sheets, and gently settled against her tender body. I kissed her face and lips. We joined quickly in our passion and soon were rocking wildly to the mad rhythms of love, our breaths and our bodies intermingling, my joy mounting with my desire, laughter now extinguishing my doubts and love devouring all fear.

TWENTY-TWO

Jyoti was dressed and brushing her hair when I woke up. I hoped she'd cleaned my hairbrush, it was full of old hair and scalp flakes the last time I used it. She smiled at me with that smile like a morning sunrise, then came over to the bed.

"Hey, sleepyhead. Did you know you snore?"

"*Damn*. Really?"

"Yes, really. Not enough to keep me awake."

"I fell asleep first?"

"Yes you did." She kissed my nose.

I got up and put on some boxers, not wanting her to see my skinny naked body.

"Would you like some breakfast? I have Cocoa Puffs."

"No thanks, I'm not much for breakfast." She stepped into my little kitchen. "Have you got any decent tea?"

"Yeah, I guess. I have Earl Grey."

"Yuk."

"There's an Oolong that's pretty good."

She said she better skip the tea, she had to catch a train and really couldn't stay. I put a mug of water in the microwave and got out a jar of instant coffee, wishing she would stay forever.

"Peter, I'll be away for a few days. My job has me traveling a lot."

"Yeah, okay. Give me your cell phone, I'll call you."

"I'll call you. That way you'll have it in your address book."

It looked like she was giving me the brush off. As she headed for the front door I said, "Will I see you at Hydra when you get back?"

She broke her stride for just a second. It wasn't much more than a hiccup in her posture, but the mention of Hydra definitely registered in her mind. That was odd, it was only a bar where she ran into me.

"I'll probably be in the Village toward the end of the week. Why don't we meet me there for a drink?"

"Great, yeah."

"I'll call you when I get back in town."

I went to my desk to get her a business card, but she opened the door without waiting for me.

"Wait. You need the number."

"I already have it, silly. Bye."

When the door closed I watched her slender figure in the video display until she stepped into the elevator. She didn't look back at my door. That seemed like a bad sign, but maybe not. Maybe she was just preoccupied with her day and everything she had to do.

After making the bed, and noting with satisfaction how the sheets had been torn up the night before, I washed the few dishes and dried them and put them away. I was determined to keep the place together in case Jyoti came back again.

After reinstalling my programs and files from a backup drive, I called up my web construction program—a sweet Drag N' Drop application I put together to save time and streamline the build—and took a look at the fisherman's site. The Quick Time video of the fish on the line played nicely. I tweaked the hue and added a sound file of waves and wind. It played very well.

After I saved the file and ftp'd it to the server, I ran an anti-spy program that removed surreptitious files from my hard drive. Even with my firewalls and virus protection, I like to sweep my computer once a day to see if anything got through. The program displayed cookies from my visit to GirlTalk the day before. Nothing unusual there, *except*. . . The latest cookie was created at one-fifteen in the morning. That was *after* I fell asleep.

Jyoti must have been on my computer while I was asleep. Now that I think about it, I hadn't shut down my computer last night, I'd been too focused on her and the kiss she gave me.

Curious, and not a little annoyed, I looked over the registry list for files opened in the last twelve hours. It's a self-monitoring program that allows me to track everything I do on the computer, so I can *undo* it if the file created a conflict. My jaw dropped when I saw over fifteen files that were opened after one in the morning.

What the hell was Jyoti doing on my computer? She'd looked at photos of Angie. Okay, maybe she was jealous and wanted to check out the opposition. Or maybe she wanted to help me find her? She could have asked me to show her a picture, I would have gladly opened the file for her.

She hadn't looked at my email, but that application is password protected, so she wouldn't have had access to it anyway. But she went to my web browser and used a tool to see what searches I'd conducted recently. The tool showed that I'd searched for references to Hydra, Night Witches, Yummy Escort Service, and Angie Andrews. So Jyoti knew exactly what I'd been looking at.

Why? What was she up to?

Who is she, really? Could *she work for Yummy Escort Service?*

I needed to find where Jyoti lived and watch her. How to get her address? I did a white pages search for an address; no luck. An online search came up empty as well, which was to be expected, I only had her first name, and unless she was a film or music star, the name wouldn't pop up on a search.

Annoyed, I considered databases that would have her personal information and were accessible on the web. Then it hit me: *the yoga class!* She enrolled in the program Becka went to. It was in a high school—what was the name of it, she'd mentioned it one time? *Clara Barton!* Becka took adult education classes at Clara Barton.

I accessed the school and without too much hassle hacked into their adult education program. The yoga class was listed. Leave it to the Board of Ed to leave confidential information unprotected. I found the student roster. There was Becka, a dozen other people, almost all women, and there was Jyoti Sumasandrum. With an address on West 10th Street, in Manhattan.

The address sounded familiar. I called up Mapquest and pinpointed the location. It was right at the corner of 12th and Eighth Avenue—the *same corner as Hydra.*

Yeah, right.

I called up a search engine and typed in Hydra. Sure enough, the same address. Either Jyoti had given a fake address or she lived in an apartment above the bar.

I went to the City Registrar of Deeds to see who owned the building. It was owned by a corporation, Yak Enterprises. Russian mob? Weird.

Wondering about the apartments above the building, I checked out rent and taxes. There were rents collected for apartments on the 2nd and 3rd floor. That made sense. But if Jyoti lived above a lesbian hangout, that didn't jibe with her working for the escort service, unless she recruited women from the bar. But that didn't make much sense, a lot of the women there were tough as nails and against prostitution.

The scheming wench spent the night with me to get into my computer, not my pants. I had to find out what her game was.

I went up to the penthouse to see if Josh or Marty had any news for me. They were eating some of Becka's new creations that smelled of cinnamon and anise. She piled a plate high with food and set it in front of me.

Josh told me, "Yo, Pete, I chatted up a couple of the girls who work the street around my bar. I was thinking they might know something about that escort service you were looking at."

My ears perked up at that, though I acted like I wasn't much interested.

"They don't like to talk about the trade, but I've given them a break now and then, letting them hang in the bar when the weather was bitch-ass cold. People remember kindness."

"How'd they show their appreciation?" asked Marty, jabbing his brother with an elbow.

Ignoring the remark, Josh went on. "Like I said, they weren't real chatty, but one girl told me she knew about Yummy and they only used new immigrants. They promise them jobs as like domestics and seamstresses, but when the girls get to New York the organization takes their passports and makes them work as prostitutes until they pay off their loan, which is pretty much never."

It made sense that Angie's credit history only went back four years. That must have been the time she entered the country and started working in the brothel. It hurt me to think that she'd started life in America on her back, but who was I to judge? The immigrant's life is tough, there are vicious people who take advantage of them. Angie must have fallen into a bad crowd and been exploited. It happened to young girls all the time.

Marty asked me what I was going to do next, cautioning me to watch the street when I went out. I told him I was going to order all my food delivered and stay locked in my place.

"I'll see that Pete doesn't starve," said Becka from the kitchen. "He can be my official taster."

I thanked her and told them I needed to think things through, so I went out on the roof and looked up at the stars. It was clear, for New York. You couldn't see the Milky Way, but the Big Dipper was suspended upside down. *Follow the drinking gourd.* I remembered the song that called the escaping slaves north. Why couldn't Angie have found a safe haven? Why didn't Gisondi and the whole police force break down Yummy Escort and all the rest of the sex clubs and put them out of business?

The world looked cold and hopeless. No one had reached out and saved my mom. No one had reached out and saved Angie. My irrational reticence had prevented me from knowing she was in trouble. I had left her alone and defenseless.

Another line of thinking caught me and wouldn't let go: *Why was Jyoti helping me?* If she was really my friend, she wouldn't go through my computer while I was sleeping. It was clear she had been playing games pretending to care about me. Could she be working for the mob? That didn't jibe with her sweet smile and with her finding me a lawyer, but still, it was puzzling.

Maybe lying and loving were what she did best. Her cooperating with me in sex was the kind of thing a woman in the trade would do. She hadn't objected a bit —wasn't that the way Svetlana would treat me?

Or Angie. If she had worked for the escort service, she might have given in to all sorts of sexual demands. That thought got me almost as down as imagining her in the Atlantic feeding the marine life.

I *had* to find Jyoti. H*ad* to know if she was just using me when she spent the night or if she really cared. If she ever offered to give herself to me again, what would I do?

Timothy Sheard

TWENTY-THREE

I slept in fits and starts that night. The littlest noise woke me up and got my heart pounding. The door to the apartment was secure, but the gate across the window by the fire escape was designed to keep a child from crawling out, it wouldn't stop a gunman from shooting me dead. I had the curtains closed, but that made me even more nervous, since I couldn't see if anybody was out there.

It made sense to add another video feed from the fire escape. I'd get out to a local electronics store and put in the second video camera as soon as I had a chance.

When the curtains started to show a hint of sunlight, I crawled out of bed and cleaned myself up. It was time to take action. Hiding in my room would just give the bad guys time to figure out how to plant my feet in cement and send me to join Angie somewhere in the Atlantic. I get seasick standing on the deck of the aircraft carrier Intrepid docked in New York harbor. Heading out to sea in a small motor boat with my hands and feet bound, I'd probably throw up and choke on my own vomit from the gag around my mouth.

If I was going to ever find Jyoti, there were two places to look. First, Hydra. She'd given the place as her address, so she probably picked up her mail there. Plus I'd seen her there, so it had to be one of her haunts.

The second place to look for her was on the web at *GirlTalk*. It had a bulletin board. If I could access the board I might find information about where she hung out.

I went to the computer and punched in the URL for *GirlTalk*. The chat room that they sponsored required a password for access. No problem, I used Kurt's hacking software and was soon in the program.

The messages were organized by topic and date. There was also a search window, which was pretty good for a bulletin board. I typed in *Jyoti,* but nothing came up. That wasn't surprising, all the postings on the list were anonymous.

I tried a query for *Hydra,* which was where Jyoti had been hanging out with friends. A long list of messages came up. Several mentioned going there and meeting other women. A few talked about issues of sexual identity. Some wrote about alcohol and drugs. It was personal and political stuff, the kind you'd expect in a lefty-lesbian community.

Hydra was definitely a favorite among the group. If I couldn't find Jyoti's address, I might find her at Hydra if I waited long enough. That could be days or weeks, which was a pain, but on the other hand, what else did I have to do with my time?

I next keyed in Night Witches. Nothing came up on the bulletin board for that word combination. There were quite a few posts that mentioned witches and witchcraft. Stuff about female mystics and ancient knowledge of healing and spiritual rebirth. New age and old age stuff. None of it made any sense to me, so I gave up reading the messages.

As a last resort I looked at the photo gallery. There was a photo of that silver-haired woman I'd seen at Hydra with a circle of young adoring women seated around her. The photo caption read, *Dr. Merriweather Sage speaking at Vassar on female identity and gender enclosure.* Whatever "gender enclosure" was all about, the students seemed to be lapping it up. I could just hear Marty commenting on it: "Another post-feminist niche ideology," he'd say. Probably right.

I keyed in an online search for Dr. Sage. She was a PhD, not an MD, with degrees in ethno-historicism and comparative geologic-biology. Where do they get these word combinations? She taught a series of classes on Historical Feminism, whatever that was, at Antioch College in Ohio. No surprise there, that place was way out on the political fringe.

I went to their web site and saw that the campus was a hotbed of radicalism. It was a far out community—clothing was optional. I couldn't imagine me walking around naked, the students would laugh at me. I've got a flat chest, skinny legs and I'm not hung all that well. Still, you had to admire them for walking the walk.

The college also had an organizational model that gave the faculty one third of the power, the students one third, and the workers one third. That was really radical. Maybe Dr. Sage wasn't such a kook after all.

Her PhD thesis was on the role of women in the underground railroad before the Civil War. So she was an historian *and* a feminist. I recalled the online accounts of the Russian female pilots who bombed German trenches: the Night Witches. The women pilots had been heroic as hell, so maybe they were an inspiration to this young generation of feminists.

If Sage had really immersed herself in the underground railroad before the Civil War, it was possible that she would want to carry the idea into the twenty-first century. Did Dr. Sage walk the walk? It seemed awfully far out—operating an underground railroad right here in the United States, but if she could teach classes in the nude at her age she was probably capable of anything.

I had seen Jyoti join Dr. Sage and her followers the night at Hydra after she ran into me. What was Sage doing in New York City if she was teaching in Ohio? I called up the class schedule and found she was on sabbattical for a semester, lecturing around the country. There was even a list of her speaking engagements at colleges around the country. And *she was speaking tonight about human trafficking at The New School!*

I decided to jump on the subway and check it out, it seemed like my best shot at finding Jyoti.

The New School auditorium was packed when I stepped in to hear Dr. Sage finish up her talk, so I had to stand in the back of the crowd. That was fine with me, I could look for Jyoti in the crowd. There were women of all shapes and sizes and types in the crowd, from cross-gender to Quaker types in wool skirts and puffy white blouses. Looking for the most part at the back of their heads, it was all but impossible to pick out Jyoti.

Dr. Sage talked about the average life span of a woman trapped in a brothel. *"Four years.* After a few years most girls are sick and dying from AIDS, gonorrhea, drug addiction and septic abortions. Suicide is common." The audience listened in grim silence, horrified at the statistics.

She went on to describe "the Swedish model." They had cut prostitution by eighty per cent by making it illegal for men to pay for sex with women or children. "It took several years to convince the police and the district attorneys to actually prosecute these men, but when they did finally make arrests and win convictions, the trade dried up dramatically."

Then she added, "And the prostitutes and children, instead of being punished, were visited by social workers and given *help* instead of degradation, which is what we need to implement here in the U.S. *today! Right now!*"

This brought cheers and a standing ovation from the audience. I had to admit, it made sense. The approach could even work in the U.S., if the law enforcement types weren't so macho-sexist

There was a period of questions and answers. Sage was patient and supportive, especially when a young woman talked about her escape from captivity. That brought out a lot of tears, and cheering when she finished her story.

When the session ended I left the building and waited across the street, hoping to catch sight of Jyoti. It was a huge crush of people, but I was hopeful I could still spot her. I knew her walk and her smile. Call me crazy, but I almost believed I would pick up her pheromones if she came near me.

Sage emerged with a bunch of groupies. I was surprised to see her walking in a slow, jerking motion, a cane in one hand, her other hand linked to a student's arm. She seemed to have some kind of muscular disorder. Could be a spinal cord injury. I didn't think it was MS, though I'm no expert.

As I tried to get closer to the group, one of them helped Sage into a cab. Another woman turned to her companion and asked were they all going out for a drink? When I heard her companion say, "Hydra," I stepped away and started walking toward the bar, hoping Jyoti would show and I'd get a chance to ask her point blank what she was really after, and praying she would give me a straight answer.

TWENTY-FOUR

Hydra was packed by the time I got there. Women chattered and listened with peals of laughter and animated faces. I never understood how women could find so much to talk about, and how they found every word so *interesting.* But the evidence was unquestionable. Women listened and responded with abandon, especially to Doctor Sage.

Sage was seated in a corner booth. She was leaning forward and listening intently to a girl with a lot of earrings in a lot of places speaking earnestly and low. Others in the booth leaned in to hear above the din.

When Ronnie, the same waitress who served me my last visit, asked for my order, I asked for a Jameson on the rocks, then added in a casual voice, "Have you seen Jyoti tonight?"

With a poker face Ronnie said, "I don't know who you mean," which was crap since she'd servied Jyoti a white wine without being given the order. Back at the bar Ronnie watched me in the mirror as she waited for the order. When she got the attention of the bartender, a fifty-ish woman with a sour puss and a don't-piss-me-off expression on her face, she leaned over the bar and whispered something in the bartender's ear. A little later the bartender stepped from behind the bar and approached me.

"Listen, mac, this is not a place to pick up women. We don't put up with that shit here." She had cool, gray, kick-ass eyes.

I told her I had no intention of picking anybody up, I was just trying to find a friend. "We had a drink together right here last Sunday. I was hoping I'd see her again."

Her eyes said *Give me an excuse to break your neck,* but she returned to the bar, leaving me on probation.

There was no sign of Jyoti. After nursing my Jameson as long as I could, I figured it's better to be anonymous than marked as a trouble-maker, so I finished my drink and went outside to wait. Besides, there was still the issue of Jyoti's home address. She'd given Hydra as her home, did she really live above the bar?

Watching the club from a doorway across the street, I noted that the building was a handsome brownstone. New York had so much great housing stock, with their ornate lintels and arched windows. This building had solid, old oak doors. No gargoyles on the facade, but still it was a beaut. Four stories of classic—

Wait a second! Hydra was on the first floor of a four story building, but the tax department only collected rents for apartments on floors two and three. So what went on at the top? Somebody had to live on the forth floor. In today's feverish housing market an apartment in the Village could rent for several thousands of dollars a month, and sell for a cool million.

Private residence, maybe? I looked at the door next to the club entrance. It led to a tiny vestibule and stairs to apartments above. I wished I knew how to break into places, but hacking computers was my only useful skill.

I tried the door just for the hell of it. It was locked, naturally. I didn't think a tenant would be dumb enough to let me into the building, even if I waited for hours until somebody approached the door. Besides, there was no buzzer and intercom. So how did a visitor get hold of somebody inside? Weird.

Through the small window in the door I could make out mail boxes on the wall. There were twelve of them. Assume four apartments per floor, that added up to three floors occupied. The names and apartment numbers were too small to read from the doorway. I took out my digital camera; it has a four-X *optical* telephoto lens, which meant that it actually magnifies the image, it didn't just spread out the pixels and make big fuzzy images.

I focused through the glass in the door and read the names. Jyoti's was not among them. The mailbox listed second and third floor apartments, but not the forth.

I was focused on the mailboxes trying to make out the names when all of a sudden I felt myself being lifted up in the air. The world went upside down, my stomach turned inside out, and all of a sudden I was lying on the sidewalk, my arm pulled and twisted behind my back. Lightning bolts of pain shot through my shoulder as the attacker twisted my arm some more.

"*What the fuck are you doing?*" she asked me. It was Ronnie, the barmaid who hadn't known Jyoti.

"Uh, yeah, sorry, I told you I was looking for Jyoti, didn't I? She gave me her address, and it's this building. I was trying to read the names on the mailboxes."

"The *names...*" The bouncer was skeptical.

"Yeah,the names!" I saw that my camera had fallen to the side walk. "Check the camera, see for yourself."

Without letting go of my arm or reducing the pressure, the bar maid bent down, picked up the camera and pressed the display command. She scrolled through the pictures without taking her eye off me. I was glad I'd emptied the card, there were no photos of Angie or any other women.

"You took pictures of the mailboxes."

"I told you, I was looking for Jyoti's name. I wanted to be sure this was the right address. I was going to leave her a note."

"This Jyoti's a friend of yours?"

"Yes."

"Why don't you call her up on the phone?"

"I don't have her cell number." It seemed better to acknowledge my ignorance than claim to have her number, the barmaid might know that Jyoti doesn't give out her number. At least to me.

"How do I know you're not full of shit and you want to mess with her?"

"Ask her yourself, she'll vouch for me."

Putting more pressure on my shoulder—it's amazing the way that excruciating pain can scramble your thought processes and make you ready to say anything to stop the pain—the barmaid pushed me down a stairs to the basement entrance of the building next door. It was dark and secluded; a perfect place to kill me and leave the body for one of the tenants to find me when they left for work in the morning.

Pressing my face and chest against the bars of the door, she made a call on her cell phone, telling somebody what I'd done and listening to a voice in an ear piece so I couldn't make out what the other party was saying.

The barmaid asked, "Should I hurt this guy?" She listened again, her hand squeezing my wrist and offering no relief. She said, "Uh huh," then, "yeah, okay, if that's how you want to play it." Finally she released her grip, allowing my arm to drop to my side. Not that I could use it any, it was numb and powerless. It felt like I'd been tortured for witchcraft on a rack.

She handed the camera back to me.

"Don't come back here. Don't take any more pictures. If you do, I'll crack your skull like a melon and leave your brains all over the street. You got that?"

"Yes, sir. I mean, ma'am. I got it."

I started walking away. Painfully. My back felt like the discs in the spine had been ruptured and the bones cracked. As I looked back, the bouncer was on a cell phone. Her hips were tilted the way the classic Greeks posed their models.

I wished I could take her picture, but knew it would be the last photo I ever took.

Once out of sight around the corner, I licked my wounds and considered what to do next. These Hydra people didn't like my snooping around. Understandable, this city is full of perverts and paparazzi. Still, the barmaid did seem awfully testy, even for a New Yorker.

There was a donut shop half way down the street with a window that had a view of the club. It was too far to make out details inside Hydra, but seated there, I was not likely to be spotted by somebody coming out of the bar. I went inside, ordered a couple of cream-filled donuts and a tall coffee, settled into a booth along the wall, and waited.

I had a first bite out of the donut and was considering the benefits of solid donuts versus cream-filled ones—you can't dip a cream filled donut in coffee, the filling will glob up in the coffee, it doesn't dissolve the way cream does—when I saw Doctor Sage come out of Hydra with two other women. The doctor's limp made it easy to spot her. The group went through the private entrance into the apartment section.

I licked some of the cream and waited.

TWENTY-FIVE

The first donut went down sweet and easy. The second didn't taste as good. Maybe the filling was spoiled. Or maybe my body was reacting to the jolt of all the sugar and trans-fat. I was debating whether or not to finish the second donut, leave it, or take it home in a bag, when Dr. Sage and four other women came out of the entrance to the apartments. The last one out was Jyoti, which was weird, because I hadn't seen her go in. Probably she'd been waiting for them before I arrived.

Dr. Sage and the other women walked east toward Seventh Avenue. I followed them staying in the shadows. They went down to the subway and waited for a northbound train. A moment later a train bound for Queens rolled into the station and I followed, taking the car behind them.

After the first stop each of the younger women reached into their purse, took out a pair of high heeled shoes and proceeded to change the ones they had on. Weird. Then they started applying makeup, going heavy with the eyeliner and mascara. That was really weird.

In Queens the women exited. As they climbed the stairway to the street I heard the *click click* of their high heels on the iron steps. Only the doctor kept her flat shoes on. Were they going to a party of some kind?

They split up when they reached the street, acting as if they didn't know each other. I stayed a block behind the last woman, confident she didn't know me. When she turned back one time I saw a taxi approaching with the occupied light on the roof lit up. I put my hand out as if hailing the taxi, and when it went by I looked after it as if thoroughly disappointed.

By the time I'd turned toward the woman she was disappearing around a corner. I hurried to catch up, able to keep on her trail from the *click, click* of her high heel shoes. Staying far back, I followed her for three more blocks. The neighborhood was industrial and poorly lit, with few pedestrians on the street.

In the dim light of a lonely street lamp I saw the young woman enter a bar. It looked like a dump. A real biker bar, with a few high, barred windows in front that made it impossible to see inside from the street. The old brick façade wasn't fashionably old, just old.

I went inside and took a seat in the corner and ordered a beer. The tiny round table wobbled when the bartender placed my beer on the it. I lifted the glass and looked over at the girl I'd followed. She was seated at the bar. When she opened her coat, she revealed a short skirt that promised paradise between her legs and a low cut top that offered to come down with the touch of a finger. I noticed she'd put on some seriously red lipstick, and that her fingernails were brightly painted as well. She was tarted up, and the few men in the pub stared at her like wolves looking at a tethered sheep.

When the woman ordered a drink, the bartender gave her a hard look and scowled. My guess was he knew which girls were approved to solicit from the bar, and this girl was not.

Two of the other women from Hydra came in, equally tarted up. They sat at another wobbly table, pretending not to know their associate at the bar. They opened their coats and revealed equally racy outfits. Now the bartender got on his cell phone, turned away from the bar and talked to somebody. I wished I could read lips.

The two men finished their drinks, got up and walked

past the bar to the stairs. A sign over the stairs read *Toilets for patrons only!* One of the men turned and looked at the girl at the bar, then at the barkeep. The bartender shook his head “no”. The man shrugged and followed his friend down the stairs.

A half hour later the two men came back up the stairs, satisfied looks on their faces. They winked at the bartender and passed through the front door, leaving the bar empty but for the bartender, me and the three women.

The girl at the bar held her cell phone in the lap and worked the keys, obviously sending a text message. She read a reply, closed the cell phone, and took out the pair of running shoes she’d stuffed in her bag when on the train. As she calmly changed back to her original shoes, the bartender watched her, totally perplexed.

The two other women in the corner changed their shoes, too. It was totally weird, like the Stepford Wives, or the Village of the Damned: three gorgeous, sexy women putting on running shoes in a seedy bar. Finished, they each slung their bag across their shoulder military style just as Jyoti, Dr. Sage and the barmaid from Hydra who’d manhandled me came in.

Jyoti saw me, stopped, looked at Dr. Sage and indicated me with her eyes. With a light nod from Sage, Jyoti came up to me.

“Peter. What are you doing in this place?”

Knowing it would be useless to claim a coincidence, I said, “I was looking for you. I thought—”

“Stay out of the way, Peter, things are going to get rough.”

Dr. Sage and four of the women headed for the stairs. The bartender asked them where the hell were they going, but the women ignored them. As he lifted the hinged section of the bar and moved toward them, Jyoti sprang at him. She landed a kick in the guy’s belly, spun around and kicked him in the back of his knee. The guy listed to the side. She kicked the other leg and he was on his knees.

Jyoti grabbed the man's ear and pulled hard. She bent down and told him if he wanted to keep his ears on his head, stay where he was and don't make trouble. Then she pushed him down on his stomach, hard.

I rushed over to her and asked what should I do to help.

"Watch the door, tell me if anybody approaches."

I went to the door, opened it and looked outside. The street was empty. There was a panel van parked in front of a hydrant with the motor running. I wondered if there were cops in it. Maybe this was a police sting and Jyoti was an undercover cop. Or maybe it was a mob guy watching the place. That would put Jyoti and her friends in danger. I told her about the van, but she didn't say anything in reply.

Minutes passed slowly, like having a teeth drilled and capped. I was so excited to be helping Jyoti, I hardly had time to be scared. Suddenly I heard cries coming from the stairwell. The barmaid emerged holding a young Asian woman in her arms. The young woman was crying. She was followed by Dr. Sage and her friends and six other girls, some white, others Indian looking. They were all crying and speaking in languages I didn't understand.

I opened the front door for them and Sage rushed the group out of the bar. The van's doors burst open and the girls were pushed roughly into the van. Dr. Sage went in last and was closing the doors as the van peeled out, leaving the smell of burning rubber from the tires behind as it rushed into the street, slowed for a red light, ran through it and sped away.

As Jyoti reached into the guy's pocket and pulled out his cell phone, he hauled back and punched her hard in the face. I leaped on the guy and wrestled him to the floor, but he had a good sixty pound advantage over me, all of it muscle. In seconds he had rolled me over, raised himself up on his knees and cocked a huge fist. Just as I put up my hands to defend myself Jyoti kicked him hard in the back of his neck. The guy's eyes rolled up in his head and he crumpled to the floor. God, I loved it when she kicked ass.

Jyoti grabbed my hand and pulled me to my feet.

"We must get out of here," she said. "They have security cameras."

I followed her outside. We ran down the street and turned a corner. Rushing along the sidewalk, we saw a black Lincoln Town car speeding toward us. Jyoti grabbed my shirt front, pulled me to her and kissed me. I could see her eyes following the Town Car as it approached us. Her body was tensed, ready to fight or flee. The car slowed, then picked up speed and passed us by.

As soon as they were around the corner, Jyoti pulled her mouth away from me and started walking rapidly down the street. I thought we should at least hold hands, but she showed no sign of wanting more intimacy. She had *great* self control. We hurried down the steps to the subway station and stepped onto the platform. The station was quiet, with only a few patrons waiting.

Jyoti went to the end of the platform and looked up the tunnel where the train would approach us. "If the train doesn't appear in three minutes, we go into the tunnel."

"*What*? Are you crazy?" I said. "We could be killed. There's no room for us down there, and the third rail has a gazillion volts."

"Six hundred twenty-five," she corrected me. "I've done it before." She looked at her watch, then at the stairs we had hurried down, anticipating unwanted company. The seconds dragged like a quiz show where death was the prize for the ones who didn't get the question right. Or even if they did.

I heard a rumble and felt a breeze on my face. It was the train, pushing a column of air ahead of it. The lights of the first car came into view. As we entered the train, Jyoti stared out the window watching, but nobody threatening came down the stairs before the conductor closed the doors and the train lurched away.

I saw a rider was staring at me, which never happens. I didn't understand why until Jyoti pulled out some tissues from her pocket and gently dabbed my lip. Then I felt the blood oozing from my mouth and tasted the salty mixture. I'd taken a good punch and didn't even know it.

I grinned.

"What are you smiling about?" she asked me.

"I like it when you take care of me."

We rode the train to Manhattan, changed trains and headed for the Village and Hydra. I wasn't leaving Jyoti's side until she told me what the hell was going on.

TWENTY-SIX

Dr. Sage wrapped her small hands around a glass of whiskey, as if the liquor might warm them. Her hands were mottled with age spots. The knuckles were swollen. Arthritis, probably.

"Peter," she said, "it is extremely important that you share with me what you know about our work."

I shrugged. "I don't know anything, really. I just went on line and poked around, is all."

Sage smiled. It was a sweet, disarming smile. Her high cheek bones and bright hazel eyes told me she'd been a looker when young. I wondered if she was born with her disability. If she had it all her life, it would have kept the boys away. That must have hurt. Probably still does.

"You were looking at the mailboxes next door. Why do you think Jyoti lives here?"

"She put this address down on her application to a yoga class, the roster is on the school's database. It's easily accessed online, the password is a simple one, all letters."

Jyoti grimaced. She was embarrassed at leaving her trail so open. I wanted to say something in her defense, but realized it would have sounded lame.

Dr. Sage was waiting for more. She had a way of looking at me with patience and understanding, like a good therapist. Her eyes were warm. Sympathetic. She was easy to trust, which made her doubly dangerous.

"When you visited Hydra, you asked about a photo of Russian female pilots. You asked if they were *Night Witches*. Why did you say that?"

"See, the way it all started was, I was looking through Angie's hard drive—"

"*Who?*" Sage asked, her face as innocent as a child's.

"Angela Andrews. She lives across the street from me."

"You were in her apartment, then?"

"No, I did it from my computer. That's a basic function tech support people perform when they check a remote site for problems. I took command of her operating system and searched the drive. The files had been erased and overwritten, so the data was splintered pretty effectively. I looked for uncommon words or phrases that repeated and that sounded provocative."

"How do you mean, *provocative*?"

"It's fuzzy logic. People usually employ basic English to send emails and write stuff in word processing programs. I wrote a program that looks for words that you wouldn't expect, and if they repeat several times in the mish-mosh of the data soup, my program computes the value of how many times they repeat versus how uncommon they are."

"That sounds like a very ingenious program," said Sage.

"It works pretty well, but I still have to evaluate each word. I found Hydra occurring several times. I did an online search for it and found this bar. And I found Night and Witches, sometimes together, sometimes apart, *plus*, I found a lot of fragments of the words together. Like, g-h-t beside w-i-t, for example. My program scans for word fragments, too. Those letter combinations suggested the words were cited together often when the drive was intact."

"You are a most enterprising young man," Sage said. Jyoti smiled at me. I hoped she was proud of me.

"Anyway, I searched for Night Witches and found, among other things, it was the name of these Russian women pilots from World War Two. Asking about the picture at the bar was to see what kind of reaction I'd get from the bar maid.

Was Night Witches, whatever they were, connected to Hydra in some way? That was my thinking."

"And *do* you think they are connected?" Sage asked, staring at me as if I was taking my final oral exams for a post graduate degree.

I shrugged again. "I don't know. The bar maid —"

"Ronnie."

"Yeah, Ronnie. He . . . *She* claimed to not speak Russian, which I didn't believe. There was no connection I could find, other than words occurring a bunch of times on somebody's hard drive. But without the actual files, I had no way to know what they mean."

Sage sipped her whiskey and watched me. I was hoping she was warming up to me, because I really wanted to be accepted in their organizations. She was trying to figure out how much I knew about her without giving anything up. I don't play that game; it was my turn to get something in return.

"Doctor Sage, I learned that the Night Witches were a courageous group of Russian pilots. They faced death over and over. If I were building a woman's organization that called for bold, dangerous action, like what you did at that brothel tonight, I can't think of a better name."

"They are inspirations to all of us engaged in social justice," Sage said.

When she wouldn't cough up any more, I went on. "One other thing caught my eye. I accessed the tax records for this building, and the company that owns it only pay taxes on the income generated by the apartments on the first three floors. The fourth floor isn't listed as rental units. Why is that?"

Sage and Jyoti traded glances. If there was a signal sent between them, it must have been telepathic, because I didn't see anything. Finally Jyoti said, "Peter, you're a nice guy and you mean well, but you're messing around with people who are a lot more dangerous than you imagine."

"Not true! I had a guy with a gun break down the door to my apartment. I saw a creepy madam strike terror in the face of a young Russian woman. And I was nearly killed by that neanderthal behind the bar. I understand perfectly what I'm dealing with."

I never should have told Jyoti about my dream of walking on the surface of Mars, she'd obviously told Sage all about me. Okay, I'm a dreamer. Okay, I fell in love with a woman I'd never actually talked with. But that shouldn't disqualify me from being accepted into their organization. And I was getting more and more sure that they had something put together.

"Let me tell you something," I said. "When I was a boy I was raised by two prostitutes: my mother and my aunt. I saw what the men did to them. And the cops. The social services? They could care less about two poor women struggling to make a living."

"It hasn't changed much," Dr. Sage said.

"My mother died of AIDS back before they had good drugs for the virus. My aunt died from a drug overdose. I know all about the ugly side of life."

Jyoti looked at Sage, who gave a slight shake of the head. Jyoti covered my hand with hers. I hate when women do that, it means they're going to tell me something you don't want to hear.

"Peter, you are a good, decent man, but you aren't cut out for our organization. You just aren't."

"Look at how I hacked into your private bulletin board," I said, pulling my hand away. "I can help you upgrade your software. I can build firewalls Bill Gates couldn't penetrate. I—"

Now it was Sage's turn to reach for my hand. Her grip on

my wrist was a lot tighter than Jyoti's. "Peter, I am grateful for you showing us the vulnerable part of our web site, I've been worried about it for some time. But romantics like you are not equipped to fight with the men who traffic women. They are no better than the guards in the Nazi death camps. Worse, in some instances. These gangs have no moral controls. No guilt or shame."

"I understand all that! I'm not a romantic. I—"

"Not a romantic?" Jyoti said. "You imagine relationships that never exist. You dream of love without ever making any of the commitments that real love requires!"

"Are you talking about me or *you*?" I said. If Jyoti was going to bad mouth my character, she was going to get it thrown right back in her face.

"Peter," Dr. Sage said gently. "You do live very much in an imaginary world. Your work designing web sites is a solitary enterprise without a collegial network. You photograph women instead of approaching them. Your view of love is dysfunctional. You are a loner with a personality that is suffocating."

"So I'm shy. *So what*? That doesn't make me crazy. I respect women. I believe they should be honored."

"No," Jyoti said. "You think a woman should be idolized. You think she should be put on a pedestal like a work of art. You aren't able to love a woman as an equal. You're so terrified of being judged and rejected, a woman in your arms is as remote as a stripper on a stage. *You see women the same way the Johns see them in the whore house."*

That hurt. How could Jyoti think I was a low life pig like the guys who go to strip joints and pay for sex?

"That's a load of crap! I would never debase a woman."

"You debased me when you watched me take off my clothes."

"That was a game!"

"It's no game when the woman isn't a partner in the planning."

All of a sudden I had a hollow, empty feeling inside me. *Could she be right? Could I really be as fucked up as the guys who slapped women around and forced them to spread their legs?* As hard as I rejected the accusation, a voice inside, like my mother's voice calling me out from behind the sofa, was saying I was dirty and despicable and not worthy of a woman's real love.

Dr. Sage softened her voice even more. "Understand me, Peter, we have to be very careful who we work with. We must have people who are emotionally whole and grounded in the real world. You do not have the qualities we require to join our organization."

I wanted to go with them to fight the scum and to free the women from bondage. Free Angie. I wanted it more than I'd ever wanted anything in my life, but my chances were slipping away. I felt myself sliding down a muddy hole into a sewer of stinking garbage.

"I'm afraid that you *must* distance yourself from us and have nothing more to do with Jyoti or this place," Sage went on. "The criminal organization knows who you are. They will try to use *you* to find *us. That must not happen.*"

Dr. Sage stood up. She held the table for balance. "Say good-bye to Jyoti, you will not see her again for a very long time. Perhaps, forever."

As Sage stood up, I said, "Just tell me one thing. Do you think Angie is alive?"

She let go of the table. "Most likely, she is not. But if she *is* alive, she is wishing she were dead."

Sage hobbled off, joining a clutch of women in the corner, where she took a seat and accepted a drink without having to say a word. Jyoti stood also. I got up and slowly followed her toward the exit. There were a lot of feminine eyes watching us as we walked through the bar. I hate being watched. I hated what Jyoti was going to do even more.

"Any chance you'll call me some time?" I asked.

She shook her head.

"Send an email?"

Same response.

"Cripes. I don't even have a picture of you. I really fucked up."

Jyoti held the door for me and followed me out. I *hated* having to go, it was just like when my mother sent me out to the empty lot across the street so she could service the johns. Or maybe just get a little peace and quiet. Now I was too old to sit and chew on a Juicy Fruit.

"Peter," she said, putting a hand lightly on my chest. I hoped she could feel my heart throbbing. "I want you to know, the feelings I showed you that night were real."

"Yeah, sure. The feelings right before you hacked into my computer and left without giving me a way to contact you."

She took my hand and looked at it, as if to see what strength there was. Or tenderness, maybe.

"It will do us no good to wish that we were in different situations. Different obligations. Wishing is your way. I have to live in the cold hard world."

I clasped my hand over hers and kissed her palm. I wanted to hold her and never let go, even while I knew she was slipping out of my life forever.

She kissed me sweetly on the lips, then she turned and walked down the street. Her slim figure seemed to melt into the shadows. By the time she was a block away, I wasn't sure she still existed.

I dragged myself to the subway, thinking about throwing myself in front of the next train. But I didn't. I waited for the train to stop and open its doors, stepped inside, sat in a corner seat with my head down and rode to Brooklyn.

Back in my neighborhood, I shuffled up to my building, took out my key and aimed for the keyhole. Just as the key turned and the electric door clicked open, I felt a steely hand wrap its fingers around my shoulder and squeeze. Hard. I looked in the glass and saw a familiar bald head reflected in the glass.

"Let's go inside and have us a chat, shall we?"

Detective Gisondi's face in the reflection of the glass door was shadowy and sinister.

TWENTY-SEVEN

Inside my apartment, Gisondi didn't beat around the bush with a lot of small talk.

"There was a fight in a bar in Queens tonight. The bartender ended up paralyzed with a fractured neck. You know anything about it?"

I told him I tried never to go to Queens. He didn't appreciate my comment. "I went to a lecture at NYU, then I had a drink at a bar and a donut at a coffee shop."

"That's it? That was your whole night?"

"Then I walked around the city awhile. I like to walk, it helps me unwind."

"A guy who had been in the bar just before the fight gave a description, sounded a lot like you." I tried to keep a poker face. "They've got a security camera."

"Really. You saw me on the tape?"

"Never mind what I saw, you were there."

"Are you arresting me?"

Gisondi fingered his earring. I wondered if that was a little accu-pressure thing he had going, like a stress relief measure. Or maybe he was trying to quit smoking.

He said, "I'd hate to see somebody with a chip on their shoulder visit you in the apartment again."

"My door is secure."

"Nobody's secure from those kind of people. You're safer talking to me. I can get you protection."

I told Gisondi I was able to take care of myself. We went around and around what I did that evening, but I stuck to my story and he didn't put the handcuffs on me, so I figured he didn't get a look at the bar's surveillance camera. But if the police didn't have the tape, that meant the mob guys did, and Gisondi was right, my steel plate and heavy duty lock would be no match for them.

After the detective left I went to the bathroom and looked in the mirror. Big mistake. The guy in the glass looked like he'd been out all night drinking. My clothes were soaked in sweat. When I reached for the faucet to run the hot water, my fingers felt like they belonged to somebody else. It was like my will went through translation software before the motor nerves synapsed with the muscles. Totally weird.

I splashed the water on my face and rubbed my skin hard with a towel that hadn't been in a washing machine for months. A man needs a maid.

In the kitchen I made a triple strength instant coffee. There was no milk, so I dropped a slice of butter into the black liquid. It made an oily film on the surface. I carried it to the computer desk and drank it anyway.

Have to work. Focus on a task. But how? I wanted Jyoti to come back and reassure me that she really wanted to be with me. I needed her to tell me it hadn't been a joke or a mistake or a favor for a friend. That she cared. That she wasn't faking it when she whispered words in my ear in a language I didn't understand.

I tried to summon up the feeling of her lips kissing mine when she said good-bye. She'd given me a tender kiss. Nothing sexy in it, but there was love, or something like it, in the touch. That kiss got me remembering how my mother sometimes kissed me. On the lips, but gently and sweetly. She didn't do it often, but when she did I always felt like I was really loved.

Jyoti is nothing like my mother. No comparison whatsoever. But her good-bye kiss had that same gentle caress. My mind kept running back to those days hanging out in the empty lot across the street from the apartment watching men go into the apartment and come out an hour or two later. Once in a blue moon a guy would spend the night. On those occasions she let me in when it got late, of course, but I had to be very quiet and stay in my little cubbyhole of a room. It was really a walk-in closet she'd fixed up for me; Aunt Allie had the spare bedroom.

When I was waiting in the empty lot to be called home, I'd look up at the moon. There's an endless fascination in the way the moon changes its shape and color. Through the seasons it shows a different light. And the stars that surround it change with the seasons, too. That was how I became interested in watching the stars. I would be sitting in a swing, if it wasn't broke, which it usually was, while the other kids would all be at home watching TV or doing homework or listening to stories their moms and dads read to them. But more often than not I was outside waiting to hear her voice say, *"Come in, Sneaky Pete!"* A part of me wished I could stay outside and watch the moon all night.

I was blown away when I realized that as the moon shrank to a tiny curved blade and then disappeared, it wasn't really gone, it was just hiding in shadow. Just like me. The moon and I were the same. We sought out the shadows and the hiding places and watched from there. Like the moon, I wanted to be invisible, but still there.

I bought a cheap little telescope from the Five & Dime and got a better look. I read in a library book that the moon was in the earth's shadow. That really got to me, I guess because I felt like I was living in somebody's shadow.

I vowed to forget Jyoti and the Night Witches and everything about them. After all, if they were into some dangerous shit, why should I put myself in that kind of situation? It wasn't as if Jyoti was going to love me for ever after, she made that clear enough. It was time to wash my hands of the whole business and get on with *my life.* To take care of *my shit.*

Who was I kidding? I still wanted to find out if Angie was still alive. I'd made a promise to myself, and it looked like the only way to find her was to convince Dr. Sage and Jyoti to let me join them, and to do *that,* I was going to have to prove that I was worthy of their organization.

TWENTY-EIGHT

When I woke up the sun was extinguishing the pale moon and fragile stars. I opened the window and looked down at the street. People were marching to the beat of their employers' drums.

There was still no milk for the coffee and nothing to eat but pasta. Not even a can of sauce. I was okay with boiled pasta and butter and salt, but no more butter in my coffee. I went up to the penthouse, knocked and entered, the door being unlocked, as usual.

"Hi, Pete," said Becka. "You're just in time for a new dish." She put a bowl on the counter that smelled of corn and honey.

"It's a native American dish," she explained, holding up the book, *Spirit of the Harvest.* "Did you know that you can go into any American city and you'll find Chinese food, Italian food, Thai food, Mexican food, but *no Native American food?"*

I confessed I hadn't noticed.

"There's a huge body of recipes and food choices from our own continent, and nobody cooks it or serves it." She explained there was a grass roots movement to establish a native cuisine and a string of restaurants and food outlets dedicated to artisinal grains and legumes and fruits.

Kurt was at his easel working on the plans for the playground. "Yo, dude, you coming to the film tonight? We've got three great Japanese horror movies."

I told him I'd try to make it but I was backed up with work. I looked at the drawing. It showed a group of children, their hands interlocked, forming a triangle.

"See, there are different patterns in the surface, depending on if you focus on the circles or the triangles or the boxes." I looked more closely and saw what he was talking about.

"If you line up with the triangle you form a perfect isosceles triangle. I thought the kids would find it interesting to see what they could make with their bodies linked together."

Amazing. Where did he come up with these ideas?

I told him I came up to bum some milk for my coffee. He got out a pint of cream. "I couldn't take that soy milk of Becka's anymore. I mean, I'm all for health and fitness, but sometimes you just got to milk the cow, you know?"

Kurt made us each a cup of strong coffee. I added a pour of cream and some raw sugar. It was divine.

I told Kurt my plan to hack into the escort service computers and try to find out where they had their brothels. I told him about my earlier date with Svetlana and that I was worried about her safety as well as Angie's. He pulled up a chair for me beside his computer and opened one of his best hacking programs, then turned the computer over to me.

I went to the Yummy Escort Service web site. There were photos and descriptions of the girls, plus several pages for men. Each escort had a bio and a series of photos. A few even had short video clips showing them dancing, usually with a partner, although some danced alone, provocatively. They weren't stripping on the video, but the implication was clear.

There was no photo or mention of Pearl, the madam who had hooked me up with Svetlana. No surprise, if she was high up in the organization anonymity would be her stock in trade. There was an invitation to join their 'Elite Membership," which was 'reserved for the most discriminating customers' who enjoyed 'special privileges'. It didn't take a genius to figure what *privileges* they were talking about.

There were drop-down menus for registering, entering

personal data, like the characteristics you preferred in a 'date.' Kurt asked if I was going to sign up, but I didn't think that was the way to go.

We took a closer look at the coding behind the Yummy web site. Their fire walls were professional grade. Kurt said that was no surprise. "The people who built the site are the same ones who hack into computers and steal financial data. They're pros."

It took us over an hour, but Kurt's software finally got us into one of the servers. I looked through the files on the drive. "It's an old Sun machine," Kurt said. "It's still got a lot of speed and power."

There were a million email exchanges of men looking for women to watch, screw and abuse in endless variations. A lot of the requests were sickening stuff. Pedophilia. Rape. Sadism. There was even a section for bestiality and necrophilia. It was a litany of abuses.

Then I found a request by a guy signing himself 'Dragon Slayer' who wanted to enter "the dungeon" and feast on the 'living dead'. *The living dead.* It sounded like a cheesy vampire-zombie flick, except this guy was for real. I pictured a medieval fortress with dark, dank catechombs, cells with iron bars and women in chains.

Kurt said, "Maybe they use paralyzing drugs on the girls. The blowfish toxin turns you into a kind of zombie, they could be into that."

"That stuff is super dangerous," I said. "Give too much, the victim dies from paralysis."

Jyoti had warned me about horrors in the brothel worse than Treblinka. This fit the bill. Dungeons and dragons...The *living dead.*

I traced the path of the email request to an account with one of the cable companies. Using their network, I traced the email back to the guy's computer, just as I'd done with Angie's. He only had the firewall and security system bundled with his operating system, so it took no more than ten seconds to access his hard drive.

I searched for credit card and bank accounts. Lucky for me, he did his banking on line. Kurt's program got me into his bank account; from there I printed out his cash withdrawals. The listing included the addresses of the ATMs he used.

"Wouldn't a guy need extra cash right before going into a brothel?" he said. I printed out the addresses of the ATM's he used, then went to an online program and printed a map of each location. There were ten of them.

"This guy really gets around," Kurt said. "He's taken out cash in every borough of the city."

I suggested we needed somebody who's more familiar with the other boroughs to tell us if any of the locations were in a sleazy neighborhood.

"What about Marty?" Kurt said. "A lot of his ambulance runs may be local, but I bet in his training he's been all over the city."

We went out to the roof, where Marty was chilling with a beer and a smoke, and showed him the map with the ATM locations.

"Any of these in sleazy neighborhoods that are likely to have a brothel?" I asked. "I'm looking for a place where they engage in some really perverted sex. Maybe violent stuff. I have a hunch this guy hit up an ATM right before going in, so I was hoping you could tell me which location would be likely to have the sort of place I'm looking for."

Marty asked, "You thinking your girlfriend is locked up in the place?"

I thought Angie was at the bottom of the ocean, but I told him I wasn't giving up until I knew for certain.

We looked over the ATM withdrawal sites. There were twelve outside his own neighborhood or where he worked.

Marty thought several of them were unlikely, they were in residential neighborhoods. "Neighbors would hear the screams and complain about the late night traffic," he said. There were two sites in an industrial neighborhood that he thought promising, one in Queens, the other in the Bronx. "Rundown and lowdown." he said. "Places that can swallow you and you're never seen again."

Stepping back inside the apartment, Kurt took out some cold beers and passed them around, asking what was I going to do next. I told him I was going to watch the escort service, there was a coffee shop nearby where I could hang out. Marty pointed out that I couldn't spend the whole day there, I'd draw attention, and the owner probably knew the scumbags who ran the brothel.

"You could sit in the McDiesel," said Kurt

"The ambulance would be better," said Marty. "Your car stands out like a black eye."

"Oh, and like an ambulance doesn't?"

"The thing is, people *expect* an ambulance to be parked waiting for a call. It's legit."

Kurt said, "How about this: we double team them. Marty and Josh watch the escort service in the ambulance as long as they can hold out. Pete and I will be around the corner in the McDiesel. If somebody comes out we need to follow, we'll tail them in my car."

I pointed out we'd need a video camera in the ambulance and a feed to see who's coming and going. Kurt proposed we use a video chat program on our cell phones to stay in touch and show what the other team was seeing.

"Could you really get your boss to allow you to park your bus in lower Manhattan?" I asked.

"Sure. The number four van is due to go in for its service. I'll take it in at the crack of dawn, when the shop first opens, it's my day off. We'll get it out in plenty of time to watch the escort service. My boss won't expect it back until the following morning.

We made a plan to start the next day, Monday afternoon. Marty would bring the ambulance to the apartment and we'd ride together to the escort service in Queens.

I didn't know how I'd acquired such loyal friends, I'd never done much for them in the three years I lived below them. This whole friendship thing is mysterious as hell.

TWENTY-NINE

I sat in the passenger seat of Kurt's car watching the entrance to the escort service from the video Marty was shooting from his ambulance, parked right across the street from the place. The smell of French fries permeating the car was a little nauseating, but I didn't say anything. We were parked at the end of the block. The street was one way, so if we needed to follow someone, they would have to drive past us.

The time dragged on slowly. The image from Marty's phone in the ambulance was good. Every once and a while Marty would ask if the person going in or coming out was important, but none of the horny men left with Svetlana or Angie. That was a bad sign, it meant they were probably in one of the brothel prisons.

"Those girls are in deep shit," said Josh, who was riding with his brother in the ambulance. "I wish we could take every one of them away."

"It's a life that ends early," I said.

"How old were you when your mom died?" he asked.

"I was ten. I went into the orphanage, then foster care, then the Juvie home."

"No kind of childhood," he said. "It's a wonder you—"

"There she is!" I pointed at the video image of Svetlana being led out of the building just as a Town Car pulled up to the curb. "Can you zoom in on her, Marty?"

"I'm on it!" Marty adjusted the video image, magnifying Svetlana's face and bringing it into focus. The burly guy who came out of Angie's building and who broke into my apartment was holding the Russian girl by one arm and the madam, Pearl, was holding the other. Svetlana staggered at the curb, but the big guy held her up like a rag doll. I could see her face was swollen from a beating, even in the small image on the cell phone. She was in serious trouble. The big guy opened the door and stuffed Svetlana into the seat, then got in beside her. The madam went around and got in the front passenger seat. The rear tires were burning rubber before she had the door closed.

Kurt started the engine and poked the nose out into the street as the Town Car blew past. We pulled into traffic, holding back two cars, and followed them east.

"Cross town," said Kurt. "Probably going to take the Harlem River Drive."

Sure enough, the big car took the entrance and jumped two lanes. They passed a line of cars on the right, accelerating hard, then weaved across to the left lane and picked up speed.

"Must be a cab driver at the wheel," Kurt said, pushing the pedal down to the floor.

"Or a cop," Marty answered on the phone. A thin line of blue smoke marked our wake as Kurt downshifted and struggled to keep up with the Lincoln.

"Better stay back, this car stands out," I said.

"Only if you get behind and smell the fumes," Kurt said, but he still kept three or four cars between us and them.

The Town Car disappeared in front of a panel truck and a big SUV. I stuck my head out to get a better view.

"If they turn off, it's Queens," he said.

"Don't count out Long Island!" said Marty, behind us in the ambulance. "Remember the Long Island madam."

The Town Car exited and took the Queensboro Bridge, making it look like they were heading for Queens. We followed them to the same seedy section where the Dragon

Slayer pervert had hit up an ATM. The Town Car parked in front of a joint that had no sign out front; not even a street number. The windows were all sealed with glass blocks and the door looked like it was made of cast iron.

Kurt dropped back and turned at the corner. We could see them through the back window. The big guy pulled Svetlana out, who this time resisted, but she was no match for him. Pearl walked up to the pub and rapped on the door. When it was immediately opened, the thug dragged Svetlana up to the entrance. She tried once more to fight going through the door, but madam punched her in the gut. Svetlana doubled over and the guy lifted her off her feet and carried her inside. The door closed behind her like the lid of a coffin.

"We should have brought your bow and arrow," I said. "And your saber."

"This isn't the movies," said Marty on the phone. "You've got to expect they're carrying, and that includes the driver and whoever's in the bar."

While we watched and wondered what to do next, I took a lot of pictures of the bar and the street. I wanted to get out and take a closeup, but Kurt reminded me that they knew what I looked like.

"They probably have surveillance cameras," he pointed out. I saw his point and stayed in the car.

A few moments later a guy pulled up in a blood red Porsche. As the car came to a stop the madam came out of the bar and walked around to the driver's side. The driver got out and held the door for her, but she stopped and pointed at the side mirror. It was bent and hanging loose.

I could see the madam's mouth going a mile a minute, she was mightily pissed. After haranguing the guy who delivered the car, she got in, adjusted the seat, then adjusted the outside mirrors. As she adjusted the angle of the rear view mirror to where she liked it, I saw her eyes reflected in the glass. For a second she almost seemed to be looking at me, but I was too far away for her to see me. Still, she creeped me out.

She ripped the car into first and tore out onto the street, accelerating hard. There was no way we could keep up with her. Besides, she'd seen our car, it would be useless to try and follow her. The ambulance might keep up for a bit, but only with the siren wailing, and Marty couldn't turn off when the madam did, that would have been nuts.

We pulled out and headed home at a leisurely pace, with Marty taking the ambulance back to base.

As the McDiesel chugged along, Kurt asked, "So what's the plan?"

I told him I needed to contact the Witches and get Svetlana out of there right away. They were our best hope.

Kurt said, "Maybe you should tell the cops about where they took Svetlana. They can handle scumbags like them."

"No cops," I said. "Trusting the police rubs me the wrong way. Gisondi threatened me with the American gulag on account of my having a telescope on the roof, there's no way I'm going to trust him with Svetlana's life at stake. The Night Witches are my best bet."

I reminded Kurt that if we didn't get in the place tonight, Svetlana would end up like Angie.

"Feeding the fishes."

"A resulka. A mermaid. I'm not going to let that happen."

"Dude, I'm not saying don't do it, I just want you to be careful. They get off on hurting people."

I wasn't thinking about me, I was thinking about what they would be doing to Svetlana in their dungeon. They may already have lined up customers to take advantage of her. This was no time to worry and wait, this was a time for action, and I was sure the Witches would see it the same way.

On the way back to Brooklyn, I suggested Kurt drop me

at home, where I could print out the photos I'd taken of the brothel. Then I'd head to Hydra and ask for Dr. Sage. Kurt thought we should call the cops, but I was doubtful they'd listen, and the Night Witches wouldn't wait for a court order.

"Don't forget they pretty much rejected you from their group," he said.

"This time they'll have to listen to me, I know where the dungeon is. They've been looking for it a long time."

As we rode down the highway, the words I'd used to describe Angie to Kurt rang in my ears. *Resulka. Mermaid.* For the first time I'd spoken of Angie like she was already dead. Like there was no hope. When had I crossed that line and written her off? Had I betrayed her?

There was still a one in a million chance she was alive. She could be in the dungeon where they had Svetlana. Or some place else. Or she could have escaped and be in hiding somewhere.

Who was I kidding? Angie was dead, just like Tasha, her body mangled and decaying in some shallow or watery grave. The image made me nauseous. Anger boiled up so hard I felt like punching out the windows.

I had only one good thing going for me. I knew where the mob had their dungeon. I could trade that information for a place on the Night Witches team. They would have to take me with them when they burst into the dungeon and liberated the women.

Kurt dropped me at our building. Approaching the door to my apartment, I unlocked the three locks, listening to the satisfying *ca-chunk* as the big lock twisted and released. I stepped inside, glad to be home sweet home. But when I entered the living room, I had a sense that something was wrong. I couldn't say what it was, but something was off. It wasn't a sound, the place was dead quiet. It wasn't anything out of place, as far as I could tell nothing had been disturbed.

But something was amiss.

Going to my computer, I tapped a key and saw it was off, just as I'd left it. I felt the side of the tower. It was cool, so no one had been running it recently.

Still, that weird feeling of something out of place stayed with me.

I started toward the bedroom. The door was ajar. Had I closed it when I left that afternoon? I couldn't remember. Just as I set foot inside, the source of the disquieting feeling crystalized: it was a faint scent. A smell of ...perfume? No. Men's cologne. Somebody had been in my a—

Pow!

Something hit me hard in the side of the head. As my knees buckled, I looked to the side. No surprise, that creep who'd broken in my door and who'd taken Svetlana away was looking at me with a deadpan face and a sap in his right hand. I thought, *interesting, he's real old school,* then I crumpled to the floor and passed out.

THIRTY

I felt a stinging in my cheek and the side of my head. Opening my eyes, I saw the beefy guy who'd let me into the brothel the day I met Svetlana standing in front of me. Apparently he'd just slapped me hard, probably not for the first time. I was surprised to note that a slap really can wake somebody up.

I was pinned to a concrete wall, my hands bound above my head, medieval torture style. The stinging in my cheek turned out to be masking the deep throbbing in my head where he'd hit me from behind.

The thug grabbed me by the hair, pulled my head away from the wall and snarled, "What'd you want to know about Angie for? Why're you bothering one of the girls?"

Here at least was confirmation that Angie had worked in his escort service. He might as well have asked, *Are you still beating your wife?* There was no escaping the assumption carried in the question.

"Excuse me?" I said. "Who?"

He slapped me hard in the other side of my face. It was like stereo, with the back of my head providing the deep bass. I felt moisture running down my cheek. I looked at his hand and saw a ring with a black onyx stone in it. Thank god they weren't diamonds, he'd have raked my skin to ribbons.

"You were asking Svetlana about a girl. Who sent you? Who you workin' for?"

"I'm self employed."

Smack! I won another prize. My face must be lighting up like an arcade. I was glad Jyoti couldn't see me, it would have been embarrassing.

"You were in the bar with those chicks, I seen the video." The goon got a lascivious grin on his face. "That little one saved your ass. She smack your butt in bed and shit?"

"She's my sister," I said.

Smack! Smack! He gave me a pair for that wisecrack. I knew I was a dead man. Images from Tasha's autopsy came back to me. I hoped Svetlana didn't end up the same way. Cripes, I hoped I didn't end up alongside her.

It looked like time to start making plans for my funeral. Not that these creeps would give me an opportunity to make out my last will and testament. Still, I couldn't help imagine what kind of flowers would be placed around my coffin, and what kind words Marty and Josh and the others would say for the eulogy. Becka would cook something nice for the wake. Crazy. Realism wasn't one of my vices.

I let my head fall back until it rested against a cold, hard surface. Looking around, I realized I was in some kind of storage room. Cement block walls, cement floor, corrugated iron roof and a metal grate at the end. There were cardboard boxes, crates and a pair of metal barrels piled chaotically at the other end. I was chained to the wall with my wrists pinned just above my head. Not high above like the cartoons of medieval dungeons. This was a kinder, gentler torture chamber.

The goon saw me looking around. "Don't try calling out, there's nobody around who cares. Anybody does hear you, they're deaf. *Got it?*"

It seemed unwise to point out that a deaf person wouldn't hear me in the first place. I looked down, saw that my ankles were chained in place as well. There was blood on my shirt and my head ached from the sap he'd used on me.

"When the boss gets here, you'll be sorry you didn't talk to me. Count on that."

My captor sat down on a nylon beach chair, lit a cigar and puffed lazily on it, not looking at me. He reached into a pocket, came out with a hip flask and took a nice pull on the flask. He let the liquid swirl around in his mouth a minute, then swallowed it. He really did watch a lot of old hard-boiled movies.

A growing tide of fear threatened to overwhelm me. I shivered. The tough guy's utter indifference toward me sent a cold-blooded message loud and clear: he was just the handler. The really bad guy would want to question me, then this guy could kill me as casually as he would stuff out a cigarette with the heel of his shoe.

A string of musical notes broke into my reverie. The melody was familiar, but I couldn't place it. My captor pulled out a cell phone, listened a few seconds, said, "Okay, half an hour," and hung up. When he pocketed the phone he looked at his watch and looked at me. He relit his cigar, no doubt figuring he had time enough to smoke it all before having to kill me.

"It won't be long," he told me, as if I didn't understand what "half an hour" meant.

I weighed the risk of spinning a story. They knew I'd asked about Angie. And they knew I'd heard the words mermaid from Svetlana. But they *didn't* know I'd hacked into their web site and learned about the dungeon. At least I hoped they didn't know.

I tried to think up a scenario that would satisfy them enough to not torture me. What could I say to them? *That I was in love with a woman who didn't know I existed? That I was looking for her body so I could give her a burial?* That sounded crazy, because it *was* crazy. More to the point, it didn't sound at all convincing. The truth would get me fucked. I needed a fanciful story that sounded true.

Gathering up what little courage I had left, I said, "Sir, is someone angry with me because I have a preference for a particular escort? Is that what this is about?"

The goon acted as if he didn't hear a word I'd said. I began a long rambling story about my innocent visit to the escort service and if I'd known how easy it was to rub somebody the wrong way I never would have engaged their services.

The guy flicked ash on the floor and blew on the glowing end of the cigar. "Save your breath, you're gonna need it when the boss gets here."

I must have looked perplexed, because he added, "You like snakes, don't ya?"

I told him they were my favorite reptile. Ignoring my remark, he put a hand around his own neck and squeezed. Then he took his hand away and pulled long and hard on his cigar, as if to emphasize the fact that he had all the lung capacity in the world, whereas I would soon be painfully short in that area.

I thought of the snake in the escort service waiting room and how it had immediately coiled around the madam's arm. It must have been a baby boa constrictor.

A boa constrictor. Great. Just what I needed. The madam was going to let a boa constrictor wrap itself around me and squeeze my chest until I suffocated.

What a gruesome way to die.

What a sadistic creep.

What the hell was I going to do?

Without a watch—I rely on my cell phone for the time—I had no way of knowing how much of the thirty minutes had already passed. I tried to listen for my heart beat. If the average young male heart beats at sixty beats a minute while at rest...was I in a resting state? The situation was ambiguous. I gave myself a rate of seventy.

If my heart beat seventy times a minute, I could listen for my heart beat, which was beating quite hard, and count them. Each run to seventy would be one minute. It was like counting cards in Vegas. I'd never done it, but how hard could it be?

I couldn't feel my heart in my chest, but the throbbing in my head was rhythmic. Was it synchronized with my heart? What was the ratio? This was a tougher problem than I'd first considered.

Feeling death's cold hand squeezing my pounding heart, I had a deep sense of loss. And regret. It was my own life I would be losing, the most precious life in the world. The little boy raised by a prostitute mother and aunt who were never given comfort or stability in their violence-soaked life. Abuse and fear were their constant companions, as they were mine. Nobody cried in our household. Nor did we find much reason to laugh.

The child, hardened in orphanages and half-way houses, would aspire to small things: three meals a day without a hand striking his face. A dresser with a drawer that wasn't regularly searched and pilfered. I never expected much out of life, though I did expect to go on living.

And to see Jyoti again. To feel her arms around me. To taste her sweet kiss. Feel her soft body pressed against mine. Speaking of Jyoti, it seemed a little odd that the thugs had broken into my apartment right after I'd met with her and Dr. Sage. Not that they were in cahoots, but it occurred to me that they could have a spy in their organization. The bar maid, perhaps. Or someone else. If the thugs had access to everything the Night Witches did, their days were clearly as numbered as mine.

I was sinking into a deep well of despair when I heard a squeaking sound. Someone was raising the gate. The thug looked at me and grinned. Had the time gone by *that* quickly? It didn't seem possible, but here was the gate going up, like a guillotine rising as they laid my head on the block and exposed my neck. I could see three pairs of feet as the gate began to lift, one of them a woman's. The Black Pearl was here with her pet snake to choke the life out of me. I hoped I didn't pee in my pants or get a hard on in my death throes. Either way, I didn't want her laughter to be the last sound I ever heard.

THIRTY-ONE

As I watched the gate of the storage compartment rise, I saw the three pairs of shoes connect to three sets of legs. Funny, the legs looked familiar. Before it was half way up, Kurt, Marty and Beka leapt into the room. Kurt had his fencing sword with him—a slender blade like the Three Musketeers used, with a fancy handle. Marty had a stout length of wood that looked like an ax handle, god knew where he picked that up, and Becka had a long carving knife I recognized from her kitchen.

As the thug jumped up from his chair and reached into his pocket for his gun, Kurt danced toward him and parried (I think that's what you call it) with the saber. The slender blade pierced the goon's hand and sank into his hip, pinning the hand. The tough guy gave out a yell, letting the cigar drop from his mouth.

Kurt withdrew the blade, drew back and thrust the tip right into the base of the guy's throat. Pressing against the neck, Kurt backed him up to the wall. Marty stood over him brandishing the length of wood while Becka, who could bone a turkey blindfolded, pressed the tip of the kitchen knife into his belly. As everyone froze for a moment in the tableau, Dr. Sage came into the room with a gun in her hand and a satisfied smile on her face.

"Key," she said to the goon.

The tough guy looked down toward his pants pocket. Marty dug in and came out with the key. He came over to me and released the chains. As my arms were freed my knees buckled and I started to go down, but he caught me in his strong arms and held me up.

"Busman's holiday for you," I said in a weak voice.

He gave me his wry half smile, as if saving my life was all in a day's work for an EMT, which I guess it was.

"What do we do now?" Kurt asked, glancing at Sage. I had the feeling he wasn't keen on killing the guy, unless it was in self defense.

"Chain him up," said Sage.

Marty secured the bastard, squeezing the cuffs tightly around wrists and ankles. While he worked, Dr. Sage asked Kurt and Becka to join her looking into the boxes piled in the corner. Most of them appeared to be stolen goods: DVD players, plasma television sets, iPads and tablets, and some fur clothing.

"I heard him say the boss was coming in a half hour. We don't have a lot of time."

We stepped to the back of the shed, where there were cardboard boxes, a wooden crate, and a pair of oil drums.

"I bet they carry the bodies out in this," said Marty, tapping one of the drums with his foot. He pulled the lid off and cast the flashlight from his cell phone into the drum. "Empty," he said." "I wonder what these stains are. They could be blood."

Kurt was going through a cardboard box. He found a manilla envelope tied with string. Inside were photographs. He held one out to me.

"Isn't this the girl you've been looking for?" he asked, holding up a photo of Angie. He'd seen my pictures of her on my desk.

I looked at the photo in the dim light. It was Angie, and it was a terrible sight. She was as badly beaten as Tasha had been. Her hands were bound behind her back and there were long twisting bruises along her chest like a barber shop sign.

Her eyes were open but they didn't seem to be focusing on

anything. They looked like doll's eyes. Dead eyes.

I held the photo out to Marty, my hands trembling. "She's dead, isn't she?"

He studied the photo. "Yeah, looks that way," he said.

Becka looked at her watch. "We better go, the others will be here any minute."

I looked at the thug in chains, wanting to kill him.

"Did you do this?" I said, my voice trembling with hatred and anger. *"Did you?"*

The goon didn't look at me or speak. I reached for Kurt's blade, but in a flash Marty grabbed my wrist.

"Don't do it, man, he's not worth it."

"Take his cell phone," Sage said. I retrieved it and handed it to her.

As the rest of us backed toward the gate, Kurt slashed the guy's belly, leaving a letter *Z*. Blood oozed onto his shirt.

Once the rest of us were out of the storage locker, Kurt, Marty and Becka lowered the grate and clamped the lock shut, then we hurried along a dark corridor. Sage led us to a little glassed in office, where I saw Jyoti standing over a skinny kid with tattoos along his arms. The kid was holding his arm like it was busted and looking miserable. Jyoti had no weapon that I could see, which explained why the tattooed kid was so down at the mouth.

I followed the others out to the street, confused about how they had found me. I spotted the McDiesel parked in front of a familiar van with Ronnie, the bar maid from Hydra, seated at the wheel. It was the vehicle the Night Witches had used when they freed the girls from the bar. I followed Marty, Kurt and Becka into the McDiesel and we took off, leaving a cloud of gray smoke and the smell of French fries behind.

"What about Jyoti and the others?" I said, looking back at the building.

"She told us to go on ahead," said Kurt, driving.

I looked at my friends. They had saved me from a painful death. Torture and dismemberment. Swimming with the fishes. I imagined myself a sort of merman, dead but still aware, drifting on the frigid ocean currents as the strange denizens of the deep took bites out of me.

Becka asked, "Are you okay, you're pale as a ghost?"

"It's post-traumatic shock," said Marty. "I've got something at home I can give him."

"Man, did you see that bastard's face when I sliced his stomach?" said Kurt, driving straight-armed as if he was handling a race car. "I wish I could've taken out my camera phone."

As we hit the BQE heading for Brooklyn, I said, "I don't understand how you guys found me."

Marty said, "I went down to your place when Becka told me what you were going to do. I just wanted to hear about it was all. Your front door was unlocked and nobody was there. That little stand with the goofy wooden statue was knocked over, so..."

"You saw signs of a struggle," I said.

"Right. I had a bad feeling, you *always* lock your door. Becka called Hydra and asked for Jyoti. She told them you were in trouble."

"I thought Jyoti was sent out of town."

"Don't ask me," said Becka. "She called me right back and told me she knew how to find you. A little while later she called with directions to the storage place."

I couldn't imagine how Jyoti knew where the goon had taken me, but there was so much about that woman I didn't know or understand, nothing seemed impossible of her.

"Man, that was a close call," said Marty from the back seat. "I would so hate to have to stuff you in a body bag and drag your ass to the morgue."

I knew Marty was trying to cheer me up with some gallows

humor, but the image of Angie brutally murdered kept intruding on my thoughts. The more I thought about her, the angrier I got.

"I need a weapon," I said to Kurt.

"Whoa, dude, not so fast. You need to stay away from those bastards, not stick your face in their business again."

"Let me borrow your sword," I said.

"You don't have any training, Pete, it's not like in the movies."

"I could take a knife. You've got knives, don't you?"

"Yeah, one or two. But picking a fight with people who are very good at killing you is just nuts."

"I don't care, I want a knife with a long blade."

Now my mind was filled with revenge fantasies. I imagined slicing the goon who'd beat me a hundred different ways. *Whack!* Off with his ears. *Whup!* His nose is on the ground between his feet. *Sssah!* His belly is flayed and his guts are hanging down like loose sausages.

And the madam, the Black Pearl, the bitch behind their whole sadistic enterprise, her I was going to cut open right beneath her rib cage. I was going to reach up and slice open her heart. I would feel the gush of hot blood as it burst from her frantic beating heart, and I would wash my hands in her blood as she died.

As we approached an exit for Manhattan in silence, I told Kurt to drop me in the Village at Hydra.

"You sure?" asked Kurt. "You're awful banged up. You need to get some rest."

"I'm going to tell the Witches where the dungeon is, and they're going to take me with them when they liberate the place."

THIRTY-TWO

I entered Hydra and took a seat in the corner. Ronnie the bar maid came to the table, took one look at me and put her hands on her hips in a posture of anger. I held up my hands palms out, saying, "Hold it right there. I'm not here to make trouble, I'm here to *solve* your troubles."

Ronnie arched a single eyebrow in a look of skepticism. I've always admired people who could do that. My aunt had the gift, but I could never get the hang of it, despite hours spent in front of the mirror as a child working on my technique.

"It's a sensitive issue. I need to whisper in your ear."

Ronnie was still doubtful, but seeing the serious look on my face, she finally leaned over and pulled her hair away from her ear. She had lovely ears. I was surprised they weren't at all hairy. Must be the hormones.

"I found the dungeon," I whispered in her lovely ear. "It's the place they hold women in bondage. Doctor Sage has been looking for it."

She pulled her head away and looked me dead in the eyes to see if I was on the level.

"You're sure?" she said.

"Yeah I'm sure. I followed them and saw them take a woman inside. That's why they came to my place and jumped me."

Ronnie took out her cell phone and typed in a text message. Finished, she asked me what I wanted to drink. I told her Irish lemonade. She went off to pour my Jameson, a double shot, neat.

I was just finishing my drink when I felt a slender hand close gently on my arm. I turned and saw Jyoti, lovlier than the harvest moon nestled in a bed of stars. Behind her was Dr. Sage, who looked me over with a practiced eye. I hoped the bruises impressed her and tried to look nonchalant about the injuries.

"Peter," the doctor began, "you should be home in bed."

"I can't do that, doc. I found the dungeon. It—"

She held up a hand for silence. "This is not the place to talk of such matters. Come with me."

She led me out of the bar and next door to the apartment buildings. We climbed the stairs to the fourth floor. As I suspected, there were apartments there.

A slim young woman lean as a whippet, with hair so short it almost left her scalp bare, opened the door silently for us. She eyed me as if I were a new species of human.

Inside, Jyoti indicated a place for me on the sofa. She sat beside me, saying, "Peter, I'm so glad you're safe." I must have looked skeptical, because she added, "I really am."

As Dr. Sage settled into a deep armchair, the young woman who'd let us in served her a cup of hot tea. The tea had a lilting bouquet that was familiar.

Sage winked at me. "Bushmills in the tea," she said. My respect for her grew a little more. "Now, then. What have you to tell us?"

I looked from her to Jyoti. "Before I tell you anything there are a couple of things I'd like to know." They sat mute, with poker faces. "For starters, I'd like to know how you knew where the place was where the goons took me. I mean, do you have a map with the location of all their hideouts or what?"

Jyoti threw Sage a knowing look. When Sage nodded slightly, Jyoti said, "I tracked you."

"You what?" I sure as hell didn't leave footprints on the sidewalk."

"I tracked you with a GPS unit. When you were asleep I slit the lining or your leather jacket and tucked it inside."

"Jesus Christ! What gives you the right—"

"Peter!" Sage had switched her calm, therapeutic look for an angry scowl. "What gives *you* the right to place yourself in the middle of one of our operations and nearly ruin the whole thing?"

"I was an asset!"

Jyoti made a sound like a horse clearing its throat. "I had to save you from a beating or worse. And then you went and let yourself be kidnapped and nearly killed."

"Hey, my locks were all in place. I don't know how they got into my apartment."

"These people defeat locks for a living."

I mumbled a little and then shut up. No way was I winning this argument. Sage drank her tea while Jyoti sat and watched me.

"You said in the bar that you found one of the dungeons," Sage said.

"You mean there's more than one?"

"Theirs is a competitive business. Look at the growth of casinos."

I hadn't thought about a whole string of torture chambers scattered across the country. They would probably be close to ports where the women and children could be smuggled in and transported quickly to their final destination.

I told them how I met Svetlana at the escort service, about my surveillance of the place and Svetlana's abduction by the madam, and how Kurt and I followed them to a seedy bar.

"You will give us the address," said Sage. "That is why you have come. Yes?"

"Yes...and no. I won't *give* you the address, I'll take you there. Tonight. I want to be with you when you free her."

"Impossible," said Sage.

"You have to! They'll kill Svetlana! We can't waste any time!"

There was a moment of silence. Sage sipped her tea, the click of her cup on the saucer the only sound in the room. Finally she said, "I believe that they will abuse Svetlana for several days. That is their habit. They will kill her when they are through with her."

"Jesus Christ, you can't leave her there with those monsters!"

Jyoti said, "Peter, you are thinking of one woman, which is understandable, but we have to think about *all* the women in bondage. If we fail, many will be hurt. If some of us are killed, it weakens our movement. There is more at stake than a single individual."

Sage added, "You must understand, we have to obtain the architectural plans from the city. We must study the adjoining streets and establish traffic patterns."

"We don't just break into a place without studying it thoroughly," Jyoti said.

Sage said, "Peter, your willingness to help is admirable. We applaud you for it. But we cannot possibly mount a successful operation tonight, and you most certainly cannot join us when we do."

"But why not? I'm not afraid of those goons."

"Then you are not seeing things clearly and objectively. These people frighten me. A man who does not fear death is disconnected from his own life."

"I didn't mean that I won't get scared once I got into the place and started mixing it up. I meant to say that I grew up on the street. I've dealt with cruel people all my life. They're not new to me. I can handle them. I won't fold under pressure."

"We don't accept loners in our group," Jyoti said.

Before I could object Sage said, "Jyoti makes a valid point. You live very much a solitary life. That is why you dream of love without expressing it to the object of your affections. We must have individuals who are emotionally healthy. Men and women who are connected to others on a deep, spiritual level. We must have that kind of bond of trust in order to do the dangerous work that is our mission."

I tried to think of an answer to her, but nothing came to mind. Nothing, because it was true. I'd been a loner my whole life. I'd never opened up to anyone. Not once. Not to a therapist or a girlfriend or to Marty or Kurt or Josh or Becka.

"You're not all that different from me," I said, fighting to stay in the game.

"Oh?" Sage looked surprised at my tack.

"You think you can create a world that's free of sexism and exploitation and abuse, but that world will never exist. That's a utopian vision. You have your dreams and I have mine."

"But there is a difference you are not acknowledging," Sage said. "We believe in trying to make the world a little better for some of its most exploited people. Just because we cannot cure all the ills society perpetrates does not mean we can't make a real difference." She paused while the young woman poured her more tea.

"Okay, I'm fucked up. *So what?* That doesn't mean I can't make a contribution. I found the dungeon, didn't I?"

Sage said, "On that point we do acknowledge your contribution to our cause."

"I don't want a medal, I want to be there when you break in. I want to know for sure if Angie is dead and buried or if she's still alive. I want to get Svetlana out of there. I *have* to be there. Tonight!"

"Even tomorrow is highly problematic," Sage said. "We will need several days at least."

Sage put her empty cup and saucer aside, sat forward on

the chair and looked at me with a face that was as sincere and affectionate as I'd ever seen, on my mother or anyone else.

"Peter," she said. "You cannot come with us, *and* I know that you will give us the location because you want your friend to be rescued, and we are the only ones who will do that."

I told myself I'd never play poker, hearts or dominoes with that woman. She read me like an open children's book. I squirmed and fought the truth, but the truth was hard as nails driven into my skull.

I wrote the address on a piece of paper and gave it to Dr. Sage. Taking out my digital camera, I added, "I have some pictures, if you want."

The young woman with short hair came and took the camera from me and the address from Sage. She withdrew to another room, no doubt to find the address on the internet and to print out the photos.

I said to Jyoti, "How could you be sure I'd wear my leather jacket?"

"Peter, it's your *only* jacket. You wear it everywhere you go, even though it has an ink stain around the pocket."

The implication leaped out and smacked me in the teeth. "You've been watching me!"

Jyoti smiled. She didn't have to say anything.

"For how long?"

"Ten weeks."

"Ten weeks! But *why? HOW?"*

Sage said, "Angie saw that you had been watching her from your window. She was very sensitive to prying eyes. Having escaped a brothel, she was exquisitely aware that one of the gang members or one of her former clients might recognize her."

"That was why she changed her hair color so often."

"Yes," Sage said. "When she discovered your prying eyes, she told us, and we began watching you. We had to know if you were one of them."

It was mortifying. Me, Sneaky Pete, the guy in the shadows who watched without being noticed, had been studied and followed for weeks. Months, even.

"Did you take my photograph?"

"Of course. Would you like to see one?"

I declined the offer, it was too embarrassing.

With a gentle smile, Sage got up and gestured toward the door.

"You have made a courageous choice," Sage said. "I will personally call you after the action and tell you about your friend."

I shook her hand. It was small and dry and very strong. I left feeling depressed about the rejection, but once I was out of sight of their peephole, I grinned all over my face.

There was no way they were keeping me out of the action. I knew where the place was. All I had to do was be there when the shit hit the fan, and try to keep too much of it landing on me.

THIRTY-THREE

Back at my apartment I found a note from Marty slipped under the door. He wanted me to knock on their door when I came in. I was beat and wanted to rest my head, it was throbbing, along with my back, shoulders, arms, legs and gut. But he'd saved my ass, so how could I refuse?

I dragged myself up to the penthouse. They were watching the Fox news on five screens and laughing out loud.

"That's gotta make the Daily Show!" Marty said at one grotesque remark from the talking head.

I told them that Dr. Sage had rejected me for joining their team, but I was going on the raid anyway.

"I knew you would," said Marty. "When do you think it'll go down?"

I told him Sage had talked about needing several days for planning it, but I had a feeling they would act sooner. Maybe even tonight.

"I'm going to stake out the brothel. I'll hang around until day break. If the Witches show up I'll jump right in the middle. They won't be able to keep me out."

I put my hand out to Kurt, who understood what I wanted. He went to his room and came back with the knife in a black leather sheath. It was around ten inches long, with scary, jagged teeth along one side and a razor sharp edge on the other.

I handed Marty a copy of my keys. "These are to my apartment. If I don't make it, you can have whatever's in my place." I wrote down the password to my computer, which Detective Gisondi finally returned. I also gave them my

ATM card and the password for that. They were somber and accepting. Good friends; I couldn't ask for more.

Marty poured me a cup of coffee and added a shot of Jamison's, telling me I needed it. Then he sat down beside me on the couch, gave me his empathetic, EMT look. "Pete, you don't *have* to do this. I mean, these Night Witches are pros, right? They've done lots of these raids. They probably have like military training and shit."

I looked back at him, eye to eye. It was weird, but I wanted to tell him everything. I wanted to spill my guts about my mom and my aunt and growing up on the streets and being in Juvie Hall. I wanted him to put his arms around me like the big brother I never had and tell me he'd be right beside me all the way, don't worry, bro', I've got your back. He wasn't saying that, but his words and his look were still comforting.

"I have to do it, Marty. It's my fault Svetlana's in that dirty place. I can't sit back and let them rape her and kill her."

"She could be dead already," Kurt pointed out.

"I let Angie get away," I said. "I'm not fucking up like that again."

Becka said, "Peter, I understand why you need to go, and I'm not trying to talk you out of it. But will you do one thing, for my sake?"

I asked her what it was. She said she wanted me to do exactly what Jyoti told me. If Jyoti told me to guard the door, I had to do it. If she told me to keep the motor running in the car, that's where I'd stay. The logic of her words was stronger than my anger and my guilt. I agreed. I couldn't deny Becka, she was pure goodness.

Marty poured me another shot of Jamesons and one for himself. We held our glasses up, clinked them and downed the shots in a gulp. The warmth spread out from my gut into my blood and throughout my body. It was a comforting feeling; a softening of the jagged edges of life. Maybe after tonight I'd take up alcoholism, it promised so much relief.

By the time I was back in my apartment my aching had been reduced, and I was ready to face whatever shit the Black Pearl and her fat-necked flunkies could throw at me. Kurt's knife was in my pocket, safely sheathed in leather. Not sure what else I would need, I grabbed a slim flashlight and my tool belt, you can never be sure when a screwdriver, pliers and wire cutter will come in handy.

Out on the street I stopped at the bodega on the corner and bought a few chocolate bars to keep me fueled for a long night. Then I jumped on the subway and headed for Queens.

Jumpy on the ride north, I stood in the subway car and watched the stations as we passed through. People on the platform appeared for a few seconds as the train rumbled into the station. You only get a glimpse of them: a face, a posture, a bag slung on a shoulder, a young couple laughing at a joke only they understand.

A lonely feeling crept over me, despite the whiskey in my system. Those laughing couples—how did they do it? How did they grow so comfortable with each other? They must have common memories and shared attitudes to be joking and laughing. Maybe it was an in-law's fussy way that got them smiling. Maybe they snuck a night together without their parents suspecting.

I never had a chance for those innocent adventures. After my mom died I lived in a Juvie Hall. That was summer camp, Nazi style. There were no mother types there, just hard-as-nails guards and social workers who expected you to fight, fail, and end up in jail. Or the morgue. If you were looking for hope you didn't check under your bed, there were only roaches and rats eating the crumbs you dropped on the floor.

When I got out I lived on the street, in abandoned buildings, flop houses with rooms that had busted doors and broken windows. You kept everything that mattered in bed with you while you slept or it was gone when you woke up. I washed a lot of dishes in a lot of greasy spoons back then. The pay was shit but the food kept me alive, and sometimes the waitresses treated me like I was a human being. That made the job worth enduring.

I could watch the waitresses and the customers through the pass-through from the kitchen. Picking up dirty dishes gave me a chance to see them close up. That was the best part. When I walked through the dining room collecting dirty dishes nobody looked at me, but I could look all I wanted. The smug suits and the tired delivery guys; the office secretaries in groups of three or four; the loner with the paperback novel and the scruffy beard. All of humanity passes through a diner sampling the food and leaving their impressions behind with the tip.

As the subway rumbled and tilted on the ride to Queens, I thought about that young couple I saw a few stops ago. When would I have what they did? Would Jyoti ever come back to me? Deep inside me was the image of her admiring me for my jumping into the fray. Her rejection of my offer to take part in the raid was just her following the company line. I imagined that deep down she wanted me at her side fighting the common enemy, and that through that fighting she would be drawn closer to me.

After the raid she would come back to my apartment and we would make wild, uninhibited love, with no tricks; no games; no hiding in the closet and watching her. Just the two of us with our eyes open, unashamedly and nakedly in love.

The subway doors opened. It was my stop, the passage to danger and to redemption.

I stepped out and climbed the stairs. Above me the night was dark, the street lights dim, with only a few pedestrians moving in silence. I got a cup of coffee from the bodega by the train station. As I walked toward the bar, the street became even emptier and more forlorn. Industrial buildings with few lights on lined the street. No yuppies had dared set up illegal apartments in this neighborhood, it was too rough.

I was glad for the desolate street. I only needed a dark doorway to make my outpost and wait for the Witches to arrive.

THIRTY-FOUR

My cup of coffee was empty and my legs beginning to ache as I stood in the dark doorway across from the seedy bar with no windows where the madam had taken Svetlana. I counted six men going into the bar during my watch. Four came out, two were still inside. With no windows onto the street, I couldn't tell if they had stayed in the bar or gone into the lower depths.

I stifled a yawn, trying to stay sharp. The sound of a car pricked up my ears. It sounded familiar. Sure enough, the Witches' van came up the street and pulled over two doors down from the bar. The passenger window came down; Jyoti stuck her head out and looked up and down the street. It reminded me of Angie when she used to look out her bedroom window every morning. The connection jumped out at me: *Angie had been a Night Witch.* That explained the women who stayed with her for a few days. Angie's place was part of their underground railroad.

She had died fighting the good fight. It didn't make it easier, but it gave her death a special meaning, I couldn't explain how.

Jyoti raised the car window, the driver killed the engine, and they sat there waiting. For what? Maybe there were more troops on the way. Or they might have someone inside who would give them a signal. Unlock a door for them. Something.

Just then a black Lincoln Town Car sped up to the club and came to a stop with screeching tires. I thought it might be some sort of VIP limo service to the place until I recognized

Ronnie, the transvestite from Hydra, being led from the car by a guy who had the muscles of a weight lifter. Since Jyoti was in the van down the street, I figured this had to be a fake delivery to get them access to the prison. They were real pros.

The fake mobster and pretend prisoner exited the car and stepped to the door of the pub as the Town Car sped away. Once the door began to open, Jyoti leapt from the van as the sliding door was pulled back and more women stepped to the sidewalk.

Silent and quick as cheetahs, five women from the van sprinted to the pub. They seemed to be wearing bedroom slippers, their feet made no sound. They all had on black turtle necks and pants, and black kerchiefs over their hair. I saw no weapons, but it was dark and they covered the ground quickly.

I hurried from my post and got to the door just as the last one was entering. As she turned to me in surprise, I winked, saying, “It’s okay, I’m a Witch too.”

The girl hurried into the pub after the others. An old guy with a beer belly and a cigarette dangling from his mouth was standing in front of a door at the back of the pub, saying to the fake delivery guy, “Nobody told me nothin’ about no delivery. Maybe I better call in and ask somebody—*what the fuck?*”

He saw the women in black coming in the door. Jyoti reached him in two steps, moving like a ballet dancer. She kicked him in his soft gut. He doubled over and she brought him down with another kick to the back of the legs and a push.

Jyoti bent down and yanked the man’s head by his hair.

“How do I get downstairs?” she said.

When the guy didn’t reply, she squeezed his throat, cutting off his airway. He opened his mouth in a vain effort to take in a breath.

"If you want to live to see the sun rise, tell me!" She loosened her grip but kept her hands around his throat.

The guy's eyes were bulging, he wasn't tough like the women. "Knock three times, two times, one time."

She released his head, turned to the last woman to give her instructions, and saw me. She told the woman to watch the guy on the floor, then knocked on the door in the proscribed pattern. We heard a heavy bolt being thrown. The fake thug pushed Ronnie roughly through the open door.

Jyoti and Ronnie jumped on the man inside the door, bringing him down in the blink of an eye. When I joined the other women on the stairs, Jyoti said, "Keep behind me and don't do anything stupid."

The team hurried down the stairs and burst into a reception area lined in red wallpaper. A man at the desk rose to his feet and reached for a weapon in a drawer, but Ronnie peppered him with blows and threw him down on the cement floor. The man howled in pain but made no effort to continue the fight. Ronnie took a gun from the drawer and tossed a set of keys to Jyoti, who hurried on down a narrow corridor.

The basement looked like an old wine cellar with rows of storage cells on either side. Each cell had a heavy wire front like a cage. The interiors were dimly lit. In the first cage I saw a woman chained to a wall, her arms and legs spread wide apart. There were whips hanging from the front of the cage. Her body was covered with welts and scabs. She didn't respond to our presence.

A woman in the opposite cell was tied to a bed on her stomach. There were whips and metal rods hanging on the wall.

Suddenly a shot rang out from one of the cages. One of the Witches let out a string of curses and fell to the floor. A trickle of blood oozed from her shoulder. I knelt and tried to put pressure on the wound.

More shots rang out. The flash of the muzzle was in the last cage on the left. The other women had unlocked and entered the first two cages. One of the women returned the fire. Jyoti flattened herself against the cage, making a thin target for the shooter at the end of the row.

She slowly inched her way along the cages. The shooter was afraid to step into the middle of the room to get a good angle on Jyoti. He tried extending his arm as far as he could and aiming at her, but Ronnie let off a series of shots and he quickly drew his arm back into the cell.

Jyoti continued to slink along the cage fronts. When she reached the edge of the shooter's cell, she waited. As the gunman paused, maybe to reload, Jyoti burst through the door of the cage, driving the shooter back. She grabbed the wrist of his shooting hand, jerked it up toward the ceiling and cracked his elbow with a sharp blow.

When he released the gun, she let it fall to the ground, pushed him back and drove the back of his head hard against the cement wall. The *crack* of his skull was as loud as a gunshot. The guy slumped to the floor, unconscious.

Pointing at a video camera mounted on the ceiling, Jyoti called out, "Ronnie, kill the camera! And get the tapes!"

Ronnie ripped the video camera from the ceiling and went looking for the computer that received the video stream.

The Witches went from cage to cage unlocking them and cutting the women loose from their chains. One young woman was delirious and couldn't stand, from blood loss or drugs or who knew what. As they hurried at their task, the wounded Witch struggled to the stairs.

I joined the women freeing the girls. In the last cage we found a metal table with gutters along the side. It looked like an autopsy table in a hospital. A white sheet covered what appeared to be a body. The feet stuck out with a toe tag on the big toe. Some sort of sick humor. It was apparent that the brothel had been offering customers a chance for necrophilia, the ultimate degradation, even after death. I couldn't help but wonder if that had been Angie's fate.

I stood beside Jyoti, frozen in horror. Was it Angie under the sheet? Svetlana? Somebody else? I wanted to look away as much as I wanted to know.

Jyoti pulled the sheet down to the waist. It was Svetlana. Naked. Dead. Her skin was pale as skim milk, except for her lips and fingernails, which were painted red. There were long serpentine bruises in a spiral across her chest and neck.

"She set the boa on her," I said, recalling the snake the madam had shown me in the escort service waiting room.

"Asphyxiation," said Jyoti. "A horrible way to die."

Stepping closer, I smelled bleach on her body. I looked at Jyoti, puzzled at the smell.

"They instill bleach in her body cavities to slow decay," she said.

It was revolting, and I wanted to go out to the street to be sick. I glanced at the guy on the floor who had been shooting at us, and son of a bitch if it wasn't the churlish manager from Artistry. He must have been the one who turned Angie in to the mob. T*he one who got her killed.*

Feeling an overpowering urge to destroy him, I took out Kurt's knife and approached the guy on the ground.

"Peter, *no!*" Jyoti yelled. She grabbed my arm to stop me. Enraged, I tried to pull away from her, but her grip was unbreakable.

"Don't make me fight you," she said in a voice suddenly soft and tender.

Letting my arm relax, I sheathed the knife, threw my jacket over Svetlana's body, and hoisted it up fireman style. Her body was as cold as a butchered animal in a meat locker. As her lolling face brushed by mine, I smelled the bleach again. They must have poured it right down her throat. It was sickening. Bastards thought of everything.

I followed the others up the stairs. Jyoti led the way, leading two sobbing young women by the hand. There were seven in all alive that we'd freed from the dungeon. Three had to be carried out, they were so badly abused.

We took the women to the van. The two in the worst condition were laid down on the seats; others piled into the Town Car, which had returned. I laid Svetlana's body as gently as I could in the back of the van and covered her with my jacket. She was still lovely.

As the van sped away, Jyoti beckoned me to join her in the car. "I'll take the subway, there's no room," I told her.

"Our rule is we stay together until everyone's safe."

"I never was good at following rules," I said.

I hurried back to the bar. The guy on the first floor had crawled along the floor to behind the bar and was trying to reach the phone. I stepped behind the bar, pulled the phone line out of the wall and dropped it on his face.

I picked up a bottle of whiskey, thinking I'd take a long pull like they do in the movies. Raising the bottle to my lips, I felt something inside me turn off. It was like a computer command that sends a message that can never be taken back.

Partly I guess it was the deaths of Angie and Svetlana. Partly it was my mom, with the AIDS and the cops beating on her and not giving two shits that she was sick and dying. It was all of that and more: it was my own pitiful, scared life, hiding from women, pretending to be loved, knowing I was not.

Inside me a pulsing fury beat stronger and stronger. I poured the whiskey over the bar, onto the floor behind the bar and the area in front. They were made of wood, old and dry. I found matches beside the register, struck one and dropped it on the floor. The whiskey ignited in an instant. The fire spread quickly along the floor and up the side of the bar. The flames danced along the smooth, polished surface of the bar.

I turned a bottle over, letting the whiskey run out into the burning pool. Maybe the bottle would explode.

I poured another bottle over the floor, saturating the sawdust scattered about. Hundreds of little torches were soon burning brightly. Happy and giddy, I dropped the match book into the flames and hurried out of the place.

I walked a long time, not wanting to show my face in a nearby subway stop. I walked and walked until I found an empty subway station miles from the dungeon. I entered the subway car. There was a homeless guy asleep in a corner. He had a foul smell and an angelic look on his weathered face. Sweet dreams at least; escape for a few hours.

I wished that I could forget what I had seen, and forget the women I had known. Why couldn't I walk alone on the surface of Mars and be done with the whole sick human race?

THIRTY-FIVE

I rode to forty-second street, got out and walked all the way down town to the Village. I thought I should let them know I was okay before going home to bed. I hoped I would dream as sweetly as the homeless guy, but the image of Svetlana on the slab kept ripping into my thoughts. It was a terrible image.

When I got to Hydra, Ronnie was back behind the bar. She smiled at me when I came in, then got out her phone and told them I'd made it back.

"Go on upstairs, they're waiting for you," she told me.

I went out to the sidewalk and approached the door to the apartment building just as the buzzer sounded. I went up to the room. Dr. Sage, Jyoti and the woman with the shaved head were sitting in the kitchen. Sage listened to someone on her cell phone, hung up, said to the others, "Lorna will survive. The bullet is removed."

"What hospital did she go to?" I asked. Jyoti told me they had doctors who treated them discreetly.

Sage turned to me. "Peter, your participation in this operation did not create extra problems, but it could very well have."

"Did you really think I'd sit in my apartment and wait to hear from you?"

"Of course not," said Sage. "Just as you did not believe we would wait several days to free the women."

I looked at Jyoti, wanting her to show some sign of pleasure in my work. Some recognition. But she didn't look happy.

"I heard on the radio the bar we raided caught fire," Jyoti

said. "Two men were taken out by the firemen. The news didn't know their condition."

As I listened to Jyoti, Sage studied my face the way social workers and cops did whenever I was in trouble. I kept silent. Why tell her what I did? They'd watched me for months in secret—where was the trust in that? And *she* was the one who had Jyoti track me with the fricking GPS unit. Let them speculate, it'll do them good.

"The fire will create many complications for us," Sage said. "It will draw the police to the cells. There is evidence enough of their criminal activities. If the news learns of it, there will be pressure on the police to investigate us."

"The police are as dirty as the men in the dungeon," Jyoti said. "They see prostitution every day and they don't arrest the *Johns.* They get their cut and look the other way."

I told them about the two cops I'd seen at the Yummy escort service and then in the police precinct when I was arrested.

"We can expect them to visit us in the very near future," Sage said. "I must return to Ohio."

"Where will you go?" I asked Jyoti.

"Out of the country."

"I want to go with you."

Jyoti sat back and crossed her arms—a bad sign.

"We have been through this before, Peter. You cannot join us."

"Why not? Didn't I do okay? I didn't freeze up. I was cool."

"Your performance was adequate," Jyoti said. "But..."

I looked from her to Sage. Waited. I began to get angry, feeling they owed me an explanation. Finally Sage said, "Peter, we have explained all this to you once before. You are not unlike the men who violate the women in the brothels. Emotionally, you are closer to them than to one of us."

"What? That's *crazy!* I'm *nothing* like them. I *worship* women."

"That's just it!" Jyoti said. "You hold women at a distance. You use them to feed your fantasies of love. You do exactly what they do, except you don't touch them. You are just like the men who watch women strip and act out sex behind a glass."

I felt a cold hand squeezing my heart. Could it really be true? Could I be as much a pervert as the creeps who went to strip clubs and whore houses? I hated the idea of using a woman like that, it made me sick. But what if I was as afraid of a woman seeing into my soul as the men who bound them and whipped them?

I was struggling with this ugly idea, unable to speak, unable to defend myself, when I saw flashing red lights outside. I walked to the window and looked down in the street.

"Four. . . No, five police cars are blocking off the street," I said. "They're going into Hydra."

The young woman with the shaved head scooped up the cups, hurried to the kitchen and rinsed them. Dr. Sage went to the bedroom and came out stuffing a laptop into a bag. Jyoti emerged with a pair of travel bags and handed Sage one of them.

"We have a way out," Sage said as they hurried to the door. "You are welcome to join us."

The young woman turned out all the lights and locked the door, then hurried to catch up with the rest of us. With no love for the cops and the Homeland Security gang, I followed them into the stairwell and down to the basement. As we passed the first floor landing we could hear banging on the front door to the apartment building.

Sage said, "The first rule of underground work is: never meet in a place without an escape route."

In the basement Jyoti pulled open a section of the wall that looked like real stone and concrete, revealing a dark, dank tunnel. "Paper mache," she explained. "This was a hiding places and escape route for freed slaves."

Sage crawled first into the tunnel. Jyoti sent me behind her, then she and the other woman followed, with the trap door closing behind us.

We crawled through the tunnel, which had a dirt floor and wooden sides and roof. My hands and knees quickly became damp. I felt the rumble of the subway to my right.

We emerged in the basement of the building across the alley. Jyoti led us to a stairwell. When we reached the first floor she opened the door to the lobby a crack and listened, then signaled us to continue up the stairs.

"I have a friend in an apartment upstairs," said Sage as we climbed the steps. "We can stay with her until the police leave."

We climbed as quickly as we could, Sage having a time of it with her disability, but she declined my offer to help. "She's only on the third floor," Sage said.

Dr. Sage had a key. She knocked rat-a tat, tat—everybody has a password these days—and let ourselves in. A light in the kitchen left the rest of the place in darkness. We settled down to wait.

"Anybody for tea?" Sage asked, filling a kettle with water. Another young woman took out cups and saucers and hunted for milk in the fridge. They were really organized. I'd never seen so much cooperation. How did they do it?

While we waited for the police to leave, Sage went over our alibi. We would all say we had been in Hydra the whole evening. She had timed and dated receipts from the bar with her signature. Women in the club would vouch for our presence. There was no video camera to contradict our story.

Sage asked if I wanted to go with them and get out of New York. I pointed out that Homeland Security was a national organization, and besides, I had my computer and all my stuff in my apartment. I couldn't see leaving it behind.

"The police have your name. They will ask you of your connection to us," Sage said.

"They can ask all they want. I was in the bar all night."

"So you were," said Sage.

The police remained in the street for hours. Around two in the morning the last of the cars pulled away. We went out to the street and went our separate ways. I walked to the West Fourth Street subway stop and headed for home, dead tired and fighting to stay awake. I didn't want to be arrested for sleeping on the train.

Entering the lobby of my building, I saw a guy on the bench with his head buried in a newspaper waiting for a car service. It was a handy spot to sit and wait, especially for the elderly.

As I approached the elevator, Mr. Head-Bowed said, "Enjoy the party, Mister Davies?"

It was Gisondi. The bastard had been waiting for me.

He stood up, approached me, said, "We *could* go to a place that's quiet and private. Just you, me, and the one-way mirror. Or if you have something in your place to drink..."

I wanted to run, but where would I go? Besides, two uniformed cops appeared out of nowhere at the front door. I held out my hands to be handcuffed. Gisondi chuckled.

"Will Jameson do?" I said.

Gisondi pressed the elevator button to open the door and gestured for me to step in.

THIRTY-SIX

Detective Gisondi sat across from me in my apartment drinking his instant coffee. I'd expected him to take me to the precinct and lock me back in the interrogation room, but he was being coy, not saying what he was going to do with me.

He looked down at a folder he'd been carrying but didn't open it. "Most of this shit's clear to me," Gisondi said, not looking up at me. "One or two pieces haven't fallen into place yet, but they will." He looked up at me. "Trust me, it will all come out."

"All of what?" I asked.

He smiled with his lips, not showing much teeth and not smiling with his eyes. You can't trust somebody who smiles with only their mouth.

"I know you've been tight with this 'women's liberation' group. Trying to get in some girl's pants. Hey, I'm not criticizing you for it. If it gets you laid, more power to you."

He opened the folder, took out a picture of the burned out bar and tapped it. His dramatic sense was right out of a television cop show. He was a cliche.

"The part I like best is the nine-one-one call tipping us off to the fire. That got New York's finest to the scene in time enough to rescue the guy behind the bar and the jerk in the basement." Gisondi bared his teeth like a dog. "We have voice recognition software. You're a geek, you know how that stuff works. We match your voice to the nine-one-one caller and that places you at the scene. We're talking breaking and entering, arson, attempted murder, and conspiracy. I don't even need the Feds on this, I can put you away for the rest of your unnatural life."

Gisondi waited for me to respond, but I said nothing. I'd disguised my voice pretty good on the phone, using a Starbucks coffee cup turned upside down and punching a hole in the bottom for a resonator. I wasn't sure it would fool the computer, but I thought my chances were pretty good.

"Do you know," Gisondi continued, "the guy in the basement had an unlicensed firearm at his side? And there were bullets stuck in the walls all over the place?" He reached out and grabbed my wrist. "What'll I find if I check you for gun shot residue? You don't have to fire a gun to collect it on your skin, you only have to be close enough to be splattered with the debris."

He looked down at my hand as if he could see the stuff with his bare eyes. Like he had x-ray vision. Trying to scare me, and he was doing a good job of it.

I wished I could ask him about the blood and the bleach and the torture tools. About the cages and what went on in them. But that would tell Gisondi I knew about them. That I'd been there. The best approach to an interrogation is to say absolutely nothing. Name, rank and serial number, that's all I was giving him. Let him dig up the rest if he could.

Gisondi switched to a kinder approach. He was bad cop/good cop all in one neat package. "Those *cages* . . ." he said, shaking his head sadly. "I've seen plenty of revolting sights in my years on the force, but those things made my stomach turn over, lemme tell you."

He tapped the file folder again, like a magician who was going to pull a rabbit out of his pocket, and stared into my eyes. To keep him from reading my face, I focused on his earring and his hand that tapped the file. That hand was open, palm down, with the finger tips resting on the table.

"Look," he said. "We know you were part of it. If I take you downtown and the DA gets ahold of you, he'll charge you a hundred ways from Sunday. The next time you put your feet down on free soil it'll be a hole in the ground."

I pictured myself lying in a casket. I needed a shave. And a haircut. And my fingernails and toe nails were in atrocious shape. I still had mud on my pants and jacket; I'd have to change into something clean and presentable before being buried.

I imagined Gisondi taking samples of the mud from my clothes and comparing it to whatever they thought I'd been doing last night.

"Not gonna make a statement?" he asked.

I shook my head.

"It's your funeral." He took the handcuffs from his belt and approached me. Before he could put them on me I told him I had something he wanted. Something he wanted badly.

Letting the silver metal bracelets dangle in front of me like he was trying to hypnotize me, he asked me what I had and that it better be good.

"I know how to find the madam who ran the dungeon where they tortured and killed the girls. She's the mastermind behind it all."

"Bull shit. You think I'm gonna believe you got close to one of the most wanted criminals in the country?"

"I have her on video. It's in my computer." Gisondi opened his mouth to speak, but before he could get the words out I told him if his brain-dead techs tried to access my computer, all the files would dissolve into mush, just like the last time.

"Ah, you got squat. She's long gone out of the country by now."

"Did she show up on any airlines or ships or border crossings?"

Gisondi slowly withdrew the cuffs, but he didn't put them on his belt, he just held them in his lap. He wanted to believe the madam was still in his reach. He wanted to make the collar.

"Talk to me."

"I can find her. I can take you to her. If you put her away it would be a big feather in your cap. You'll get a promotion. You'll get your face on the front page of The Post. You'll—"

"I get the picture. How're you planning to perform this feat of magic?"

"That's my little secret."

"Oh, no you don't. I gotta be in the loop."

"If I tell you how I'm gonna do it, I won't have anything to bargain with."

"Hey, I'm the only thing standing between you and prison time."

Gisondi had a good poker face. Whatever he said, whether in anger or with a promise of help, he always sounded totally sincere. He was good.

"The only thing I'll tell you is it's about a car. Give me twenty-four hours to get the address. As soon as I find her I'll call you and you can make the arrest."

Gisondi didn't like trusting me, but I stuck to my guns. Without giving me a little rope, she would slip through his fingers, and Gisondi knew it. In the end, he gave me twenty-four hours.

"I'm keeping a man watching you the whole time."

"I expect no less."

After Gisondi left, I felt exhaustion take hold. I triple locked the front door, turned off all the lights and fell into bed, muddy clothes and all. I figured I'd wash up in the morning. If I lived to see the daylight.

THIRTY-SEVEN

When I got up the next morning I washed my face, changed my clothes and thought about what to do next. I figured there was a tap on my phone and my email, but the help I needed was just above me. I climbed the stairs to the penthouse, knocked once on the door and stepped inside and joined Kurt at the kitchen table. Becka was making buckwheat pancakes with bananas.

"Did you know that buckwheat isn't really a wheat? It's a fruit," she said.

Kurt spread mashed blueberries on top, added a dollop of honey, and dug in. I found a plate of cakes in front of me and practically inhaled them. When the first mouthful exploded in flavor, I realized how hungry I was.

"I put some fresh ginger and a little pineapple juice in the batter," Becka said.

"You need to open a diner, not a food cart," I told her.

Marty came out of the bedroom stretching his long arms and yawning. He poured himself a mug of coffee and joined us at the table.

As Becka served him pancakes she looked at me. "Pete, what happened to you, are you okay, you look worn out?"

I told them I was okay, I'd had to crawl in the mud to make a getaway. I explained about the cops raiding Hydra and the apartments above the pub. I finished with my chat with Detective Gisondi.

"That was smart, buying some time," Marty said. "Are you going to split? Hide out in Mexico or something?"

Becka slapped Marty in the chest. "Be serious, Peter isn't

running away, that would just make him look guilty." To me she said, "Do you really think you can find that woman when the New York police and the FBI haven't?"

"I'm not sure how hard they've been looking, at least the New York cops," I said. "But yeah, I think I've got a shot to nail her ass."

I reminded Kurt of the time we watched Pearl chew out the driver who delivered her red Porsche. She pointed at the side mirror and practically split his lip slapping him up and down. She was *boiling*.

"Don't you think getting that bad boy fixed is her number one priority?" I said.

"I'm with you!" said Kurt. "We hit up the Porshe dealers, ask them has anybody brought that model in for repair?"

"Right. You have friends in the auto repair business, right?"

"Sure I do. My friend Teddy deals in new and used parts all the time. He could call around and ask if anybody has the parts in stock. The conversation could go to how expensive it is to keep parts like that on the shelf, how often do you get a call for one. . ."

"Doesn't every customer with a Porsche want it fixed while they wait, no delays accepted, etctera, etcetera," Marty added.

"The color would be a give-away," Marty added. "Didn't you say it was a deep ruby red?"

"Yeah, with a gorgeous clear coat," said Kurt. "There can't be more than a handful in the greater New York area. Lemme call him.

Kurt opened his cell and selected the name. "Yo, Teddy, my man, how's my favorite grease monkey? What, the McDiesel? It's running great, thanks to you! Hey, how about helping me build a solar powered car? From the ground up." Kurt listened to a string of expletives. "C'mon, you're a genius! You could make a lawnmower run on grass clippings!"

Kurt got down to business, explaining that he needed to track down an Asian woman who just had or was trying to get her Porsche side mirror fixed, could Teddy call around and see did anybody work on the car?

Kurt listened to some questions, then swore that he hadn't knocked the woman up and he hadn't abused her car, he was tracking her down for a good friend who needed to find her.

"I'll explain it all to you when we come over. Yeah, an hour, we'll come to your shop. Yeah, cool, thanks."

Kurt grinned full face as he closed his cell. "Car nuts are a brotherhood like no other," he said, holding out his plate for more pancakes.

Kurt pulled up to a garage with a battered sign on McDonald Ave. The blue faded letters were barely legible: Misty Motors. When I asked Kurt how the place was named, he told me it was the owner's favorite movie.

"Anything Clint Eastwood did, he has it on DVD," Kurt added. We entered the garage area, a dark, cavernous region that smelled of motor oil and auto paint. Behind a wall of plastic sheeting somebody was laying a coat of paint on an old T-Bird.

Teddy was a short Italian-American with black curly hair who looked a lot like Dean Martin, only shorter and with crooked teeth.

"Jimmy Dean!" the mechanic called out. He wiped his oil-stained hands on a rag stuck in a back pocket and shook Kurt's hand.

"Teddy," Kurt said, "this is my friend Pete. He needs help."

"Any friend of Jimmy is a friend o' mine," Teddy said, giving my hand a strong shake and a clap on the arm.

Puzzled by the name Teddy called him, I looked at Kurt,

who explained that when he and Teddy were in line to pick up their high school diplomas, they'd given the announcer fake names as a joke. Kurt was Jimmy Dean, Teddy was Lance Armstrong. The principal stared daggers at them afterward, but they were out and there was nothing the bastard could do to them.

"So, you're trying to track down a new-ish burgundy Porsche Carrera with a busted side mirror. Is that it?"

"Yup."

"And the owner's not carrying your baby or any shit like that?"

"She's a pimp who keeps girls in prison until they pay off their smuggling fee, which like never happens. They end up with AIDS and Hepatitis and stuff. She's poison."

I added that the madam had ordered my girlfriend killed, plus a friend of hers, plus another girl.

"What are the cops doin'—getting laid and lookin' the other way?" Teddy asked

"It looks like it," I said. "There's a detective named Gisondi who claims he's on the case, but I haven't seen him arrest anybody, so. . ."

"So we're on our own, like always," Teddy said. "C'mon inside."

He took me to a tiny office crammed with car manuals, books of parts orders and invoices. His desk was overflowing with paper.

"Okay, here's how it works. I called the three Porsche dealers in the city and asked if they had the parts she'd need to fix the car. No surprise there, none of them did. I talked trash with the service manager, complaining about this and that, and he told me somebody else asked for the same part just the other day."

Kurt and I exchanged looks of satisfaction.

"I didn't think he'd give up the name to me. I mean, why

should he, we're not cousins. But I have his name and the shop address, so the rest is on you."

Kurt and I thanked Teddy for his help, got back in the McDiesel and took off in a cloud of sweet smoke.

On the way to the dealer we discussed our strategy, debating whether to come up with a story or to go with the truth. We both agreed that the truth was stronger than anything we could make up.

"Any chance you have that picture of Angie from the storage locker?" Kurt asked.

"I've got it, why?" I said, pulling it out of my jacket pocket. Kurt thought the picture and the story would convince any decent guy to help us track down the monster who did that to Angie.

At the Porsche dealership we parked in the lot, the attendant there sniffing the air and asking Kurt what was he running under the hood.

"It's a German diesel retrofitted to run on vegetable oil we harvest from the fast food joints," Kurt told him.

"Far out. Free fuel."

Inside Kurt found the service manager, a lean guy with dirty blonde hair and a square jaw who didn't seem to open his mouth real far when he talked. His shirt had "Sid" stitched into it.

"Teddy called you for us about a side mirror for a Porsche," Kurt said.

"I told him I could get him the part, take about a week. Coming from Germany."

"We don't actually need the *part,*" Kurt said. When the fellow gave him a quizzical look, Kurt asked if we could talk to him in private about a delicate matter. Sid took us to an office only slightly bigger than Teddy's but considerably neater.

"This better not have anything to do with gray market

parts," Sid said, closing the door. "I don't play that kind of game. We stock strictly Porsche-approved parts."

I handed Sid the picture of Angie, dead. We waited for him to soak up the image.

"This is—*was*, my friend Pete's girlfriend. A nasty piece of work they call the Black Pearl runs a string of whorehouses. She smuggles the girls into the country and forces them to work until they pay off their debt, which they never get to do. Any girl who tries to get out, like this one and two others that we know, is strangled to death by the madam's pet boa constrictor. They end up in a landfill or the bottom of the harbor."

Sid handed the photo back to Pete. "You're looking for payback, I guess," he said.

"We're gonna let the cops handle that. The problem is, they can't find her, she's gone into hiding. But I figure her car means more to her than anything else. You had somebody order the part recently. I bet it was her."

Sid keyed in his computer, scrolled through a couple of screens, read a few lines of text. He looked over the screen at us.

"I could lose my job for doing this. You know that. Right?"

"We know," I said. "But if you had known Angie or Svetlana you'd see that—"

"Spare me the closing argument, you had me with the snake," he said, holding up his hand. He hit a button, the printer chattered and it spit out the information. Sid handed it to me, saying, "When they get ready to pass sentence on her, I want you to tell me. I wanna see the bitch's face when they put her away."

I took the paper and read the name and address. It was in the Bronx address, and in a toney section, too.

"Have you finished the car?" Kurt asked.

"Nope. I told her it would take a week, ten days to get it, but she jumped up and down and demanded I have it shipped overnight express. Cost a shit load, but she didn't care. Paid cash. I finished the job and my driver drove it up there this morning."

"I'm surprised she let anybody drive it after her man smashed it in the first place," Kurt said.

"Me, too. She was gonna pick it up, but then she called and said she had a business appointment she had to keep and I should deliver it to her garage and leave the key with the valet. So I did."

We thanked Sid and got back in the car and headed for the Bronx. I couldn't believe how decent and helpful the service manager had been. When I told Kurt my surprise, he said, "Dude, most working people are pretty cool. Give them a chance to do the right thing, they'll usually do it. It's usualy the ones dreaming of getting rich and moving out of the old neighborhood who'll stab you in the back."

I had to agree. And I had to wonder.

As we headed for the Bronx we planned our next move: talk to the parking attendant, try and scope out where Pearl lived, and see if we can determine if she's at home. If she was at home, we'd have to decide, call the Witches or the cops. The Witches weren't a revenge-kind of crowd, so calling them didn't look like it would get us anywhere. That left Detective Gisondi.

"If he's on the take, he won't arrest her, he'll take *us* in," I said.

"May-be," Kurt said,

"You have your blade with you?"

"I keep one in the trunk," he said. "Why?"

"I'd like to run it through her black heart."

"Dude, I'm not into killing somebody. Besides, she'll have bodyguards with guns, remember?"

I admitted the chance of coming upon Pearl unarmed

and defenseless was zero. That left calling Gisondi with the address and hoping he would do the right thing.

What choice did we have?

THIRTY-EIGHT

As Kurt pulled into the parking lot in the Bronx, a young Hispanic man with baggy pants, boots with the laces untied and a sweatshirt came out, rolling his shoulders as he walked like a seaman.

"Wha's up, you guys can't read?" He pointed to the large sign, black letters on an orange background stating that the parking lot was for the exclusive use of the residents of the building: *Violators will be towed at their expense.*

Kurt had the McDiesel in park. He stuck his head out the window, his hair wild and curly, and said, "Hey, man, I'm not looking to park, I'm just after some enlightenment is all."

The young man came up to the car, sniffed the air, cocked his head to listen to the motor. "That's not too rough for a diesel. Is it a Mercedes?"

"Volkswagen," Kurt told him. "I did some modifications to it. It's got a light-pressure turbocharger my buddy and I sort of designed ourself."

"For real? What're you burning?"

"Fast food grease. Most of it's from the local Chinese. Some Burger King, some, McDonalds."

"Sweet. Fuck BP and Mobil and all of 'em."

"You said it."

Kurt pulled the car into an empty slot, got out with me, went over to the booth where the attendant had a chair.

"Nunio," the young man said, slapping Kurt's hand, then mine.

Once we introduced ourselves, Kurt told him how we were looking for the owner of the red Porsche. I handed him the photo of Angie. Nunio looked at it a long time.

"My cousin got lost three years back. The cops said she ran away, but I didn't buy it, she was real close to my gran." He looked at the picture once more, almost like he knew her. In a way, he did.

"Tell me what you want."

"We just want to get a look at the car, make sure it's the one we're looking for."

"You ain't gonna try t' boost it or key it or nothin'?"

"No, we won't touch it. We just need to find this woman."

Nunio told us the number of the parking space. We looked around the lot. It was empty of people.

"Five minutes," Nunio said. "Then you're history or I get fired," he said.

We promised and walked into the garage. It was not well lit. Pillars divided the lines of cars, our feet echoing on the cement floor just like in the movies. The Porsche was parked nose in in a corner spot. The curving red surface reflected the dim light.

"Sweet ride," Kurt said as we stood looking at the car. "It'll do one-sixty, easy. The wing keeps the rear end from lifting off from the air foil effect." He turned to me. "Is this the car you saw?"

"It's hers," I said. "Check out the stuffed snake on the dash."

Kurt pointed to the wall where the nose of the car pointed. It had the owner's apartment number. We were in luck.

We thanked Nunio, made our way back to Kurt's car, and drove out to the street, parking down the block.

"Let's scope out the lobby," Kurt said.

We walked past the front of the building. There was a doorman who opened the door for a resident. It was obviously locked to all intruders. We couldn't think of any excuse to get past him, and we didn't believe our picture of Angie would do the trick, doormen were always getting hit up with sob stories. They were a jaded bunch.

Kurt said, "If we knew the layout of the apartments we could figure out which window to watch. You could get your telescope and try and see is she home."

"I can't see buying flowers and trying to deliver them," I said.

"No, probably not."

We decided to grab some lunch and decide what to do next. We found a Tex-Mex restaurant with a bilingual menu. Typical New York. I ordered a burrito, Kurt had the fajitas.

"You have to call in the cops, Pete," Kurt said when his sizzling chicken and vegetables arrived on a hot iron skillet.

I twirled some noodles around my fork and didn't say anything. I knew he was right, but I hated to give up the idea of killing the Black Pearl myself.

"You want revenge, okay, I understand that. But you don't have any way of getting to this woman, and even if you *did* meet her face to face, the chances are better she'd kill you rather than you killing her. Not to mention you'd end up doing the time."

I stabbed a meatball, wishing it was the Pearl's body and I was piercing her over and over again with Kurt's fencing sword. I imagined hearing her beg for mercy, screaming, choking on her own blood as I ran the blade through her throat.

When I finished the plate of food I gave up the fantasy of killing the madam myself and agreed to call Gisondi. I took out my cell and punched in the numbers. He was at his desk—a lucky break.

"What d'ya got?" he said. It sounded like his mouth was full of food. Must be his lunch break as well.

"I found her."

"Who?" Gisondi said, trying to play dumb.

"The Pearl. The head of the gang that killed all the women,

who do you think?"

There was a moment of silence. He was chewing on something, the news or food, I couldn't tell. Finally he said, "You're shittin' me. In one day you track down a suspect the Feds have been looking for for like years? How the fuck'd you do it?"

"I'm psychic."

"Don't bullshit me, the DA still wants to bring charges against you."

I told Gisondi about The Pearl's red Porsche and how she went ballistic when her driver busted the side mirror. "I figured she'd make fixing it a priority, so I called around to the dealers and found out who fixed the car and where they delivered it."

"No shit. You'd make a good cop if you could pass the psych exam," he said. "Gimme the address, I'll be there in half a shake."

I told him the street address and apartment number, adding that Kurt and I were in a Mexican restaurant just down the street. He told me to stay where I was and not interfere, and hung up.

We got the bill and went out on the street to wait for the calvary. I wanted them to be blowing the bugle.

THIRTY-NINE

After an ice age of glaciers crawling across the continent, Gisondi pulled up in his unmarked car. He stepped out with another detective. A pair of uniformed cops followed him into the lobby, while another duo went around to the back.

The doorman took a long look at Gisondi's badge, then he followed the cops to the elevator. That was all I needed.

"I'm going in," I told Kurt.

"Hey, man, maybe you better leave it for the pros."

No way I was going miss the arrest. I still had Kurt's double-blade knife in my pocket. If I was supremely lucky I'd catch The Pearl coming down the stairs and stab her in the gut. I'd aim the blade up into her heart and twist it, making a tear so big, she'd be dead before her face hit the stairs.

Trouble was, the door to the lobby was locked, you had to be beeped in. Pissed, I wished I knew how to pick locks. The glass door was thick enough for a bank teller's post, no way I'd be able to break it, even if I had the tools to do it.

Then I remembered Nunio. I went out and jogged around to the parking lot entrance at the end of the building. Nunio was at his post reading a graphic novel. I explained what was going down.

"What you wanna do?" he asked.

"Let me in the door to the building. You've got a key, right?"

"Course I do. I got to let delivery guys in and shit." He looked around the lot, saw that no one was around.

"I do this for you one time," he said, walking to the door half way down the lot. "Anybody asks, you went in the front door. Okay?"

I thanked Nunio as he unlocked the door, slipped inside, found the stairs and went up three steps at a time. It was a long climb, thirteen stories, and I'm no jogger. By the time I got to ten I was panting for breath and my legs were rubber. But my anger had me pumped. I crawled up the last three floors. At thirteen I rested on the landing. No sense going one-on-one with a bodyguard when my legs wouldn't hold me up.

Opening the door to the hall a crack, I stuck my head in and looked around. Down the hall a uniformed cop was standing guard outside an apartment. The door was wide open. There was no sound.

My curiosity was overpowering; I had to know if they caught her. I strolled down the hall trying to act nonchalant, like I lived in the building. I was going to rubber neck as I passed the open door, maybe ask the uniformed cop what was happening, but when I got to the door Gisondi was standing in the living room and he spotted me.

"Jesus fucking Christ, how did you get in here?"

"A lady walking her poodle let me in."

Gisondi waved for me to come into the apartment. "She's not here. She split, and you're the one tipped her off."

"Me? You're crazy!"

"Oh, yeah? Check out her TV."

Gisondi pointed to a big flat panel mounted on the wall. It had split screen capability. There was a small window in the corner showing the parking garage. The video camera there provided a feed to the apartments so owners could check on their car, make sure there was nobody lurking behind a pillar waiting to attack them.

There was the Porsche, with two uniformed cops looking in through the windows. The Pearl must have seen me and Kurt casing the car.

"Fucking A," I said.

"No shit, Sherlock," Gisondi added.

It was a disaster of my own creation.

Gisondi instructed one of the uniforms to get the surveillance tapes and bring them to the precinct. Then he told me, "We're going down to the station and go over this step by step. I want to know *everything* you know about her and her operation. *Everything!* I was *this* close to arresting her and *you* blew it for me!"

I rode in the back seat of his car. At least I wasn't handcuffed. Yet. Not that a future in forced labor wasn't staring me in the face. Without a line on where The Pearl had gone, I had no bargaining chips to offer Gisondi, and it was obvious he wanted to take out his frustration on me.

As I rode to the police station, a thought out of left field hit me, hard. Yeah, okay, it looked like The Pearl made me and Kurt examining her car, but what if that wasn't what happened? What if somebody warned her that the police were closing in and she turned on the video feed to throw the police off the track?

What if it was *Gisondi* who gave her the warning, and he was making me the scapegoat? Riding to the precinct took on a whole new layer of dread at the thought that the detective was dirtier than I had ever imagined.

FORTY

Gisondi left me alone in the interview room. It had the same puke green colored walls as they do in Brooklyn. An eternity passed. I started getting more and more pissed off, at myself more than anyone else. We'd been so close to nailing that monster's ass; so fucking close. I should have known there would be surveillance in the garage. But who loves their car so much they stare at a monitor all day long? I never owned a car, I'm a New Yorker, cars are for rich people and tourists from Jersey.

Eventually Gisondi came in looking unhappy, but misery was his raison de'tre, nothing new there.

"Did you see her on the video tape from the lobby?" I asked.

"Yeah. She split right out the front door. Big sunglasses, floppy hat, hand bag big enough for a week at the shore."

So fucking close.

I went over the sequence of events. Talked to Nunio, looked at the car, went over a plan with Kurt in the restaurant. Called Gisondi, waited a long time for the fuzz to arrive.

A very long time.

"What was the time on the tape that Pearl took off?" I said.

Gisondi gave me a hard stare. "That Sherlock Holmes shit again?"

"Hey, I'm the guy who found her. I did it once, I can do it again."

"You better not be bullshitting me," he said, taking out a notepad and flipping through the pages. "And I want that video you took of the madam outside the escort service."

I swore I'd make a DVD for him as soon as he let me out.

"Let's see," Gisondi said, looking through his notes. "She passed through the lobby at three twenty-seven." He looked up at me. "So what?"

"I spotted her car at two-forty, but she didn't leave for close to an hour." Gisondi avoided looking me in the eye. "What time did I call *you?*"

He rummaged through the note pad, stalling. Finally he said, "Three twenty."

"Ha!" I almost blew him out of his chair. "She left after I called *you,* not after I scoped out her car!"

I watched Gisondi's face as he tried to come up with an explanation that didn't implicate him.

"So she was planning her getaway," he said. "She's an expert at staying ahead of the law, no surprise there."

"You have to let me go," I said, bringing him up short. When he asked why, I told him I was going to find her and hold her until the cops arrived.

"No fucking way I'm letting you out of here. You think you're some kinda bounty hunter?"

"You don't let me go, I'm telling the DA all about the timeline, it's quite an interesting coincidence."

"You threatening me?" GIsondi stared bullets at me and he had the gun to go with it.

"I'm just telling you the facts of life. Spring me, I get you the prize. Keep me, you've got a lot of shit to answer for."

Gisondi folded his notebook and put it in his pocket. He looked even more surly and miserable than the first time we met. It was a pleasure making him suffer.

"You got twelve hours."

"I can't guarantee I'll find her in—"

"Twelve hours. Then I pick you up and start laying out the charges."

I got out of the police station as fast as I could go. Kurt was waiting across the street in the McDiesel, a worried look on his face.

"What's the problem?" I asked, diving into the passenger seat.

"A couple of cops gave me the once over when they walked past. I was afraid they'd make me take an emissions test, with the odor and all."

"I thought you said the car passed inspection."

"It did, but that was before I modified the engine." He hit the pedal and hustled down the block. "You want to go home?"

"Thanks, Kurt, but we're not going home, we're going back to Pearl's apartment."

Kurt shifted into third and punched the radio. Hip hop rhythms resonated from the speakers in the trunk. I couldn't help moving a little to the beat. It cheered me up. If a kid from the streets could hit gold, why couldn't I be lucky just one time?

When we reached Pearl's apartment building I asked Kurt to park across the street just up from the parking garage entrance. It was in front of a fire hydrant, but I promised to watch for a cop so he could pull out before getting a ticket. As I got out and walked toward the garage entrance, Kurt knew what I was thinking.

"Dude, you really think she's coming back for her car?"

"Keep the motor running, it's our only shot!"

I went to the garage. Nunio was reading his illustrated novel. He was surprised to see me again.

"Man," he said, "I thought the cops would be sweating your ass in a cell for like days. Dogs on a leash and shit."

"I got out on a twelve hour pass. Listen, Nunio, did the cops put a lock on the Porsche's wheels?"

"No, they just blocked it off with that yellow tape. Always makes me think of fly paper, ya know?"

"I see what you mean. Listen, what time do you go off duty?"

"Eight o'clock."

"Is there another guy who mans the booth?"

"Nah. The night porter is supposed to watch the video, but he's a boozer, so, you know."

Nunio saw me look deep into the garage toward the Porsche.

"What, you think she's coming back? You *crazy*?"

"No, I'm obsessed. There are some things I feel like I can't live without. It's my disease. I'm hoping she feels the same way."

"But the cops will be watching for her soon as she drives away."

"By morning it'll be painted black, the top will be cut off and it'll be a convertible. Or she'll run it into a covered truck and have it on a boat heading for the Orient."

I went back to Kurt in the McDiesel and told him I was going for coffee and sandwiches. As soon as a legal parking spot opened up, he should take it, we might be there a long time.

FORTY-ONE

I looked at my watch. Three a.m. I was in the driver's seat, Kurt was sleeping peacefully in the back. We agreed to switch off every hour, but I was giving him an extra sixty minutes. The madam was my nemesis, after all.

We lucked out with a spot just down from the entrance to the garage with a good view of the entrance. Every once in a while somebody would pull up, flash their garage door opener, the big metal door would slowly lift and they'd go in.

All of a sudden I heard the door coming up. There was no car in the driveway going in. Once the door was half way up, I saw the low profile of the Porsche in the dim garage light, its headlights out. Couldn't see the driver's face, the light was reflected on the windshield. There was a chance she'd sent one of her bodyguards to drive the car through the police tape, but I knew I had to hope it was her behind the wheel and take my best shot. I couldn't keep up if the driver got the sports car into the open street, she'd run red lights and whip around other cars and be out of sight in seconds. The McDiesel was reliable, but slow as molasses.

I started the engine, threw the car in gear and hit the gas. With the diesel engine's ample supply of low end torque, the car shot out of the parking spot as the Porsche passed under the garage door and moved up the driveway.

Kurt jerked his head up as I started the car.

"Get your seat belt on!" I yelled. "You got air bags?"

"Yeah, I retrofitted a pair from a Chrysler. Why do—"

Kurt saw I was still accelerating hard as the Porsche came up the driveway. He threw his hands up in front of his face as I aimed the McDiesel straight at the low slung sports car. My lights were off, too, so the driver didn't have a chance to dodge me. I rammed the McDiesel into the passenger side just as the car crossed the sidewalk. Imbedded in the car's side, we screeched and slid into the parked car on the street just past the entrance. The sound was awesome. Our air bags exploded as we hit, obscuring my view.

I poked my head around the air bag as it began to deflate. The driver's side of the Porsche was pinned against the parked car, no way she was getting out. I put the transmission in gear and turned off the engine, leaving the big car locked onto the Porsche. Even if the driver was able to reach the door, it wouldn't open.

Leaping out of the car, I ran to the front of the Porsche and looked in the window. It was her. The Pearl, mistress of horror. Her air bag had gone off, too, so she was awake and totally pissed off. She was cursing and pushing the door and banging on the car. She tried to lower the window to crawl out, but the electronics were out, so the window wouldn't come down.

"Dude," Kurt called out. "She might have a gun."

"Let her try and shoot me. I'm fucking in charge."

I calmly reached into my pocket, took out my cell, and dialed nine-one-one.

The Pearl continued to slam her hands against the door. She even got her legs up in the air and was banging them against the glass trying to break it. Let her cut her legs on the glass, I thought, she's not getting out. I took out the big knife, unsheathed it, and held it up so she could see it. The streetlight glinted off the long blade.

I ran the blade in front of my throat in a pantomime of slitting. The message was loud and clear: *If you get out of the car, bitch, I will slit your throat and laugh as you choke on your own blood.*

The Pearl shook her fist at me and continued to kick at the glass. It splintered and blew out. She poked her head and shoulders out, but I was on her in a heartbeat, my knife inches above her face.

"Go ahead, make my day," I said.

Pearl looked at the knife, thought better about her chances and crawled back into the car.

In the distance I heard a siren calling.

FORTY-TWO

I was shaving after taking a long hot shower. New blade in the razor, new can of shaving cream. Even a fresh wash rag and clean towel. *All hail the new and improved Peter Davies!*

Shopping at the pharmacy earlier in the day, I'd even been tempted to buy dental floss, but felt, hey, this wasn't an extreme makeover, this was a *modification* of a solid structure.

I'd been going over and over what Jyoti and Dr. Sage had said about my being more like the Johns than like a healthy guy who respects women. It was an ugly fact, but it was a fact I couldn't deny. I fed my fantasies on them, just like the men who paid for their bodies.

It all had to do with my hiding behind furniture as a child and hanging in the empty lot all those years. Living in orphanages and in the streets and in Juvie hall watching to see who was going to hit me or take something from me or lie and say they cared and then walk away from me. It was my conditioning, just like Jyoti said. I was fucked up and I was gonna always be that way.

That was when it hit me. Man, I am so slow to see things sometimes. The 'me' who is still hiding behind sofas or sitting alone watching people go by and wishing they'd take me with them—that was still *me*. That approach to the world was still a part of my psyche. It fueled my urges and tamped down my fears. Watching and being unseen still gave me a thrill. That much hadn't changed.

*But, f*or the first time. . . I mean, for the very first time in my short, sorry life, I saw this tiny space between *that*

Sneaky Pete—that scared little boy waiting for his mother to call him home—and a grown up, confident Peter who *liked* himself. Who was proud of his accomplishments, and, let's face it, I'd done some pretty kick-ass heroic type stuff. A Peter who, with all my flaws, was still worthy of love.

Shaving in the mirror and reflecting on all the crazy, dangerous things I'd done to try and save someone in trouble, I began to feel as if my frightened self was this ugly skin, full of warts and boils and pus and stink, that repulsed everyone around me. For as long as I could remember this ugly skin had covered me and defined me. But now there was this little gap in one small patch of skin, and I could see healthy, clean, good skin beneath it. And I had this uplifting sense that I was going to eventually peel that whole ugly skin away and come out clean and smelling fresh like in the TV ads for body soap.

It wasn't going to happen overnight, and there would be patches of ugly skin stuck to me for a long time. Maybe for my whole life. But I had a hint at the Peter I could be. No, that I *was.* And that glimpse of a lovable Peter had me singing and laughing and feeling so happy inside that I winked at my image in the mirror.

When I was fresh as a daisy, hair slicked back and breath fresh with minty mouthwash and a solid gargle, I went up to the penthouse. Becka was in the kitchen whipping up a mix of savory dishes, Josh was strumming his electric guitar unplugged, his cap on sideways, his long fingers dancing over the the strings, Kurt was drawing at his easel and Marty had five different shows on as many screens.

As I came in, they all looked up and grinned stupid grins, with my face being the stupidest of all.

"There's that kick-ass guy!" Becka called from the kitchen. "Give him a drink, somebody!"

Kurt got out a bottle of Jameson as Becka set out glasses and ice. We all laughed and drank and toasted ourselves. To have friends like this, it was a dream come true. For years I wished I could fit in with some social set, and here I had a band of brothers and sisters all along, I'd just been too blind to see them.

"I'm watching baseball in Japan, the US, and Puerto Rico," he said, "plus Irish football and soccer."

"Yo, dude," Kurt said, pouring a glass of Guiness for me. "We whipped that nasty piece of shit's ass good, didn't we?" He took another pull from his glass. "You guys should've been there. Pete rammed my car right into her Porsche, but even better, he pinned the driver's door against a van so she couldn't get out. It was like demolition derby meets Mission Impossible."

"Can you forgive me for wrecking the McDiesel?"

"The McDiesel will rise again!" Kurt said, lifting his glass high. "My man Teddy's already got it in an alignment shop. They're gonna pull it out until the body's lined up straight as an arrow, then the body shop'll replace the front end. Should only take a couple of weeks."

"I'll pay for the work," I said.

"It's insured. Besides, I told reporters from The Post and the Daily News that it was Teddy who got us on to the madam's address, so he'll get mucho free advertising in the press."

We were just starting a second round of food and drinks when the door opened and in she walked, slim and lovely and overwhelmingly desirable. Jyoti smiled at me with her radiant eyes. She was luminous. I wanted to kneel down and worship her. I wanted to grab her and pull her into one of the bedrooms.

Becka offered her food and Kurt, a drink, but she declined.

"I've come to say good-bye," she said.

"You're leaving town?" I said, my heart skipping a couple of beats.

"I'm leaving the country."

"Where?"

"I can't tell you that." She paused, seeing my disappointment. "It's not that I don't trust you, Peter, I do. But we have security practices that work for us."

"Need to know," I said.

"I knew you'd understand."

Jyoti stepped toward the door to the roof. "Can I talk to you for a minute outside?"

I would have crawled out the door on hands and knees, even if I were heading for my execution. With Jyoti gone, my life would be empty.

We stood by the parapet looking out at Manhattan. It was a clear evening, the steel and glass glinting in the sun bending west and preparing to go to her rest. A plane heading west after the sun sparkled as it reached for its cruising altitude. Was she going by plane or car or ship? To Europe or South America or Asia? Was there any way I could find her?

Unable to take the silence any more, I said, "The night you slept with me, it wasn't real, was it?"

She looked out across the city, not meeting my eye at first. "My life is complicated, Peter. It's hard to explain."

"Feelings are simple. You love somebody, you hate somebody. What's the confusion?"

"The *confusion* comes when you love an ideal." She looked my way. "And when you commit your life to that principle. It forces you sometimes to play a role you may not want to." She looked away. "Or you may, without intending to."

"So you're saying you really love me but you had to use me to get what you needed."

"That simplifies things a bit."

"The simplest programs work the best." I looked at her face, her hair, her throat and shoulders, wanting to burn the images in my brain so sharply they would stay strong and clear forever.

"If you do care about me, why can't we stay in contact? I have an anonymous email program that will let you write me and nobody will trace the station where you sent it."

I waited for the blade of the guillotine to drop. She was cutting me off, I was sure of that. I expected a clean chop to the neck.

"Peter, do you remember what I told you the last time we spoke, that you are more like the Johns who use the women than you are like us?"

"Of course I remember. It's burned into my brain like a brand on a steer."

"I want you to know, I don't disrespect you for being who you are. We are all products of our conditioning."

I grabbed her by her upper arms and pulled her close, just like in the movies.

"Bullshit. That view doesn't leave any room for changing who you are."

"We can't escape Pavlov's dog."

"I'm a man, not a dog."

"We cannot extinguish our basic fears. We can only act in spite of them, with great effort." She pulled away from me. The distance was a Grand Canyon. A thousand light years of empty space.

I had only one chance to get her to soften. I didn't have much hope she'd stay with me or make a commitment, but it might convince her to stay in touch, or at least call me up when she was in town.

"Jyoti, there's something I want to tell you." I was glad I'd showered and shaved and looked half way presentable.

I told her about the epiphany I'd had today. I told her I was on a path to a new identity. I admitted I was still basically fucked up and scared shitless of her and all that other intimacy crap, but I was learning how to connect and I was beginning to take a chance on opening myself up to others.

Jyoti listened, looking into my eyes like she was staring into a pool and trying to see the bottom. When I was done, she leaned forward and kissed me tenderly, but also in a sexy way. Then she smiled and told me she believed in me. That she always had.

"So you'll call me when you get back to New York?"

"If I live to return, yes, I will. I promise," she said.

That was rough. Yes, she wanted to see me again, maybe even believed in my impending 'makeover.' But she could easily be killed during her next raid, leaving me nothing but the chance Dr. Sage or Ronnie would give me the bad news.

It wasn't a living happily ever after ending, it was something else. Something better. Harder. Something painful and bitter sweet.

I kissed her again, longer and deeper, and then she pushed me away with a laugh.

"I can't miss my ride, Peter. I'm sorry."

I followed her back into the living room, saying, "I'll ride with you to the airport."

"The car's waiting for me downstairs."

Jyoti said good-bye to the group. Becka handed her a paper bag with food. "For the plane," she said.

I walked her to the elevator. One more short kiss, the doors opened, and she was gone. But not forever. There was hope for me for love, without hiding in the closet watching.

I went back inside and poured myself another drink.

"I'm getting stinking drunk," I said. "Who's with me?"

Cheers and plates of food and claps on the back. I settled on the couch with Marty and Kurt, caring not a whit who was playing who or what the rules were or the score, but just enjoying my friends and imagining Jyoti on the plane, leaning back, ear buds in her pretty ears—and, oh, if my tongue could only sing in that lovely ear—and knowing she was thinking of me now and then.

Ah, life: what is more real than the promise of love?

THE END

As a reader I enjoy stories about characters who struggle with the major social issues of the day and fight for justice. As a writer I try to weave social matters into the story while keeping the characters the focus and the heart of the novel. Having worked as a nurse for over forty years and finally retiring, my story milieu is always linked to health care and the people struggling to provide it, a dramatic environment and an endless source of stories.

Through my work with the National Writers Union I have been able to mentor many writers, helping them find their voice and become published. That work has been and continues to be as satisfying as were my nursing duties. And with my publishing company, Hard Ball Press, I am putting working class writers into print so that their voices and their experiences can be enjoyed by many.

My work and my life have benefited from too many friends and colleagues to name them all. But along the way my dear wife Mary has been an invaluable resource and an encouraging voice, and I am grateful for her patience and her years of support while I hid myself away to write. My friend Dave has provided much fodder for my stories, as well as enormous help in bringing my books into print; I couldn't have created my stories without his help, and I am thankful for his many contributions. Thanks also to Marc Abbott and Rebecca Malchie for their critiques and encouragement at our writing circle as I struggled with this magical adventure of writing.

TITLES FROM HARD BALL PRESS

The Lenny Moss Mysteries, by Timothy Sheard

THIS WON'T HURT A BIT

SOME CUTS NEVER HEAL

A RACE AGAINST DEATH

SLIM TO NONE

NO PLACE TO BE SICK

A BITTER PILL

HARD BALL PRESS Standalone Books

LOVE DIES, A Thriller, by Timothy Sheard

MURDER OF A POST OFFICE MANAGER,
A Legal Thriller, by Paul Felton

SIXTEEN TONS,
An Historical Novel, by Kevin Corley

WHAT DID YOU LEARN AT WORK TODAY, THE FORBIDDEN LESSONS OF LABOR EDUCATION,
nonfiction, by Helena Worthen

www.ingramcontent.com/pod-product-compliance
Lightning Source LLC
LaVergne TN
LVHW091121080826
845145LV00008B/2000
* 9 7 8 0 9 9 1 1 6 3 9 0 8 *